# DEAD AHEAD

DETECTIVE PAUL CULLEN MYSTERIES BOOK 3

PAUL PILKINGTON

First published 2021

This edition published 2023



Published by Fast Paced Fiction

Paperback ISBN: 978-1-915367-29-7



This novel is written in British (UK) English. British English words, spelling (favourite, colour, etc.) and grammar are used throughout.

Cover design by Jeanine Henning.

*For my family and loyal readers*

## ALSO BY PAUL PILKINGTON

Detective Paul Cullen Mysteries:

Long Gone

Fallen Angel

Dead Ahead

Deep Sleeper

May Day (coming 2024)

Emma Holden Trilogy:

The One You Love

The One You Fear

The One You Trust

Standalone Novels:

Someone to Save You

I Heard You

For Your Own Protection

# PART I

# PROLOGUE

*Previously...*

Detective Chief Inspector Paul Cullen gripped tight hold of the overhead hand support as the packed tube train jerked to a stop. Caught off balance, he swayed against the back of the woman who was pressed close to him and mouthed an embarrassed sorry as she turned. Even just a nudge couldn't be pleasant from a six foot three, fourteen stone police officer. Apology accepted, his attention turned back to the young man he'd been watching for the past few minutes on this journey below London towards Euston.

'Apologies for the slight delay as we're held at this red signal,' the driver announced to the weary commuters over the inadequate speaker system. 'Hopefully we'll be on our way in the next minute or so.'

The young guy under Cullen's informal surveillance was standing against one of the glass panels, next to the sliding external doors, side-on to Cullen. From his vantage point across the carriage, the guy wearing a bright yellow construction worker style jacket looked to be really tight in to a young woman, his crotch sometimes brushing against her rear.

There weren't any signs that they were a couple – no communication between them, no acknowledgement of the other's presence.

*Was the physical contact deliberate?*

There was a time when the thought wouldn't have occurred to him. But not any longer. Such crime was a real problem on the tube network. London was no different to any other city on the planet, where heaving rush-hour transportation systems offered the chance for offenders to take advantage of the sardine-like conditions on trains, trams and buses and 'have a feel'.

And there were plenty of people, a depressing number, ready to use the conditions on the London Underground for their own pleasure. Almost always men. Young, old, suited City types, t-shirted tourists, teachers.

Operation Archangel had caught all these, and more.

Involving hundreds of uniformed and plain clothes officers from the British Transport Police stationed across the capital's rail network, Operation Archangel had been remarkably successful at identifying and catching offenders who had previously got away with crimes that had often left women and girls terribly traumatised.

For Cullen, as lead officer for the operation, the sheer number of offenders who had been caught in just a few months was satisfying and depressing in equal measure.

*Was this another one?*

The Northern Line train jerked again as it rocked forwards, not far now from Euston. This was Cullen's daily commute. An early-morning, packed overground train from just outside the M25 into Waterloo, then onto the tube. Alighting a couple of stations early, the fifteen-minute walk from Euston to the British Transport Police Headquarters in Camden Town gave him precious time to think – about ongoing cases and, in recent months, about how to rescue his marriage.

But at least there was now a solution in sight.

The train emerged into the bright light of the station as Cullen kept his gaze on the man. People around him began shifting into position for disembarkation as the train's brakes screeched. The guy bent down and picked up the rucksack that had been wedged between his feet. He was about to disembark.

If he were going to do anything more obvious, it would be now.

Cullen allowed people to slide past on either side of him as he watched on. The adrenalin was really pumping now. He craned his neck to keep eye contact with the two people. The train juddered to a stop and, just before the doors swished open, it happened.

The guy's hand snaked around the girl's waist and slithered up her right side. The girl, still with her back to him, reacted instantly, shrugging him off in disgust and shrinking back into the carriage, her face full of shock.

The guy darted out through the doors, not looking back.

*Cullen had just a few seconds.*

He moved quickly towards her as the rest of the passengers exited. 'That man, did he assault you?'

She was tearful. 'Yeah, he did.'

'Don't worry, he won't get away with it.' Cullen looked across at the doors. He didn't have much time. People were already boarding. He shoved a hand into his pocket and placed the card in her palm.

'Paul Cullen. British Transport Police. Call me.'

And then, against the tide of incoming commuters, he headed for the doors.

A MASS of people flowed onto the train, clutching bags, carrying cases or hand in hand with children. For such a large guy, Paul Cullen weaved impressively around the incomers, apologising as he went, his chances of disembarking and giving chase to the offender slipping away. Just as he reached the exit, the warning beep to indicate the doors were about to close sounded. He threw out a powerful hand, jamming the door open. Straining against him, the door resisted. Cullen thrust his right foot to its base, bumped the doors open with a shoulder charge and, as expected, initiated the tube train's safety mechanism. All the doors slid open.

He slipped out onto the now quieter platform. The eyes of an old couple directly ahead were on him, their anxiety obvious, before they looked away.

'Oi!'

Cullen looked up as a visibly annoyed underground worker strode towards him, wagging a finger.

'You can't do that.'

There was no time to show ID. 'Paul Cullen. British Transport Police. Operation Archangel.'

'Oh,' the man said, standing down and flushing crimson. He would be well aware of the high-profile police operation. 'Well, sorry, officer.'

'Sorry to delay the train.'

'That's fine... can I...'

But Cullen was already off down the platform, flashing past the still-waiting train. The man he was pursuing had long gone. But there was still a chance of intercepting him, even if he had left the station – especially with his distinctive jacket.

But the opportunity faded with each passing second.

Soon the guy would disappear into London's maze of people-filled streets.

Fortunately the platform was quiet, and Cullen hit a strong stride around the corner and up the well-worn stairs: quicker and quieter than the escalator. All the time, he scanned for the neon jacket.

Out on the concourse he reached the back markers from the train he had just left. A young family of American tourists talking excitedly about the day ahead, an old man, head down, with a walking stick, an elderly lady with a wheeled shopping trolley, bumping it over the uneven floor.

No sign of the man in the neon jacket.

Still he remained hopeful that he was closing the gap, given that the guy didn't know he was after him and presumably wouldn't be hurrying.

*But if he were getting on a bus directly outside the station...*

He picked up the pace.

This was one reason why he loved his job.

You never knew what was coming.

He scanned through the ticket barriers and out into the main concourse of Euston's mainline overground station, trying to spot the guy. To the right the electronic boards displayed the 9:35am train to Edinburgh, via his home town of Wigan: the town made famous by George Orwell, with its tiny pier by the canal.

He thought momentarily of Sarah. She would be packing at home, finalising things for her journey up North.

*Would she ever come back?*

Snapping his attention back to the task at hand, he spotted two uniformed officers over to his left.

Both recognised him as he approached.

'Sir.'

Cullen didn't have time for pleasantries. 'A young black guy in a bright yellow neon jacket. Like a construction worker's. Have you seen him?'

'No, sir.'

'He would have come up the escalator from the tube. Just a minute or so ago.' He looked around again, but still no sign.

*Unless he'd connected with another service underground...*

*Damn.*

Both officers shook their heads.

'Sorry, we've just been helping a member of the public who'd lost their bag. Really sorry, sir.'

Cullen suppressed his frustration. It wasn't their fault. 'Can you put a call out, black male, short dark hair, yellow neon jacket, in the vicinity of Euston station or travelling from there on the network. Suspected sexual assault. He might be long gone, but worth a shot.'

'Of course.'

Cullen moved towards the exit, still not giving up, as he heard one of the officers radio through his instructions.

And there he was, exiting the pastry shop just outside the station, paper bag up towards his mouth.

Cullen jogged towards him, adrenalin pumping, his prey in his sights. He waited until the man was just a few metres away and came at him from the side.

'Hey!'

The man's head snapped sideways in surprise.

'Police. Can I...'

The man shot off at speed, as if the words had been the firing of a starting gun in an Olympic sprint final. Cullen gave chase, nearly slipping on the bag that the man had dropped to the ground. He thought he heard a girl shout from behind as he pursued the man down the path from the station, but he couldn't really take anything in apart from his goal.

'Stop!' he shouted, as the man increased the distance between them.

But he didn't stop. Didn't slow. Bemused passers-by turned their heads as the two men continued their race.

The man, now quite a few metres ahead of him, approached the always-busy main road that traversed the front of the station, connecting North London's great main-line stations of Paddington, Euston, St. Pancras and King's Cross. The crossing was on red, with several people waiting as four lanes of London traffic rushed by.

Maybe he would turn sharp left and continue along Euston Road, try to outrun him and then dart into one of the many side roads.

But Cullen thought not.

He would more than likely take the much riskier but potentially more effective option.

And he did.

The man hardly slowed as he reached the crossing, darting through the first lane of traffic, a black taxi blasting its horn as it was forced to push on the brakes.

Cullen, too, reached the crossing, heart pounding as he stood shoulder to shoulder with the other pedestrians, willing the lights to go green. But they remained steadfastly red.

Another horn blared as the man stepped out in front of a delivery van coming from the opposite direction of the taxi, this time causing the vehicle to come to a complete stop. Several horns blared as the ripple from the sudden braking stopped three more vehicles behind.

Cullen dismissed the idea of traversing the dangerous road himself. He didn't fancy his chances. And a dead detective would never catch the guy. Surely the lights would turn any second.

But not in time.

Maybe the man's attention had been taken up by the near-miss with the van, or maybe he was so close to the other side that his concentration had faltered.

He stepped right in front of the oncoming red double-decker bus.

With a shocking thud the man was propelled along the road from the force of the impact, skimming along the tarmac and into the oncoming traffic. An articulated lorry coming from the opposite direction crunched over his body, dragging it under its large wheels as it slammed to a halt with a hiss just in front of them.

Surely the guy had no chance.

Screams rang out from both sides of the road as Cullen hurried up to the vehicle. The man's body – he was just a boy, really, maybe nineteen or twenty – was crushed and broken, his face twisted in shock.

There was blood everywhere.

Cullen cradled his head, supporting the limp and lifeless neck, looking him in his dead, questioning eyes. Just seconds ago this person had been in flight, full of life, but now the lights were out.

'Oh my God, oh my God! He's... oh no, please no, please...'

Cullen turned to see the girl skid to a stop, feet from him. It was the victim from the tube carriage.

Her face was twisted in despair and shock, tears gushing. A woman who had been waiting at the crossing instinctively placed an arm around her back.

'He's dead. Oh my God, he's dead!'

Cullen didn't understand.

'My boyfriend!' the girl screamed at him, her eyes flaring with sudden anger. 'You've *murdered* my boyfriend!'

~

SHAZNEY POWELL SCREWED her eyes tight shut as the coffin that contained her beloved Tyrone was carried into the church by his four friends.

She didn't dare open them, for fear that the sight of the wooden box would send her spinning to the ground.

'He can't be dead. He can't be dead. He can't be dead.'

She felt her father's arm around her back, and it did give her comfort. She let her head drop onto his shoulder, and she sobbed uncontrollably into his neck.

'Don't worry, Angel,' her father said. 'The man who did this to Tyrone. The man who did this to you. He's going to pay a very heavy price. A very heavy price indeed.'

# 1

*Monday morning*

RODNEY MARSHALL HAD BEEN DRIVING trains for the past forty years. It had been his dream job, ever since his father had taken him to Clapham Junction in the 1960's to watch the steam engines power past, all heat and movement. It had seemed like their heavy breath was from a living organism, rather than a man-made machine. The sights and smells were seductive and he knew then that he wanted to be a part of it.

With steam fading into history and heritage tours, he'd grown up to take charge of high speed diesel and electric trains, criss-crossing the country at over one hundred miles an hour, from Scotland to Cornwall and the East Coast.

It might not have had the romanticism of steam, but there was nothing he had loved more than being in control of them.

Until one day everything changed.

The day he killed the young boys.

The morning had begun like any other. He'd arrived at his base, then London's Euston station, in good time for his early morning ride up to Edinburgh.

The early Spring weather had been perfect. All clear skies and promising sunshine as they powered out of the capital, heading purposefully north.

He shouldn't really have been working that day. It was his wedding anniversary, and his wife Jane had not been happy that he'd picked up an extra shift at the last moment.

But he hadn't wanted to let the company down. He had old fashioned values, about going the extra mile to help out. He promised to make it up to her.

*If only he had put his wife before his work...*

The journey had passed by uneventfully until the train had left Newcastle, skimming by the shimmering sea along the Northumbrian coastline.

For a moment he had been lost in the beauty of it all, the serenity of the vista.

Later he hadn't been able to remember how long the daydream had lasted.

Seconds probably.

That's what the inquest had concluded beyond reasonable doubt.

That's what his advisors from the union had pushed for. His representative had made the case well.

*Rodney is an extremely experienced and professional driver.*

*He has a thirty year unblemished record.*

Had.

It must have only been seconds, but travelling at one hundred and twenty-five miles an hour, seconds of a drop in concentration made a difference.

At least that's what the voice in his head kept telling him.

No matter what the police, the inquest, his colleagues, or his family said.

He'd snapped out of his imaginings just at the moment the boys playing on the track realised that there was a high speed train careering downwards them.

He blasted on the horn and initiated the emergency brakes.

But it was a futile effort.

Within seconds the locomotive ploughed through the four children, scattering their bodies like pins at a bowling alley.

The hard, sickening thuds against the nose of the vehicle reverberated around the cab like death knells.

Rodney knew they had no chance.

But once the train had come to a jolting stop, some distance down the line, he disregarded protocols, exiting onto the trackside and running back towards the point of impact.

His chest tightened as he cleared the last of the carriages.

He'd hit and killed animals before, more times than he cared to remember, but never a human being. It had happened to colleagues, mostly suicides.

He'd always feared such a situation.

And here is was - in the most horrifying of guises.

A group of boys.

Children!

It took him what seemed like a lifetime to reach the point where the boys had lost their lives so brutally.

He spotted the first body just off to the side of the rails, bent and twisted.

Another body lay some way down the line, face down.

He knew they were both dead, but still he checked up close, immersing himself in the true horror of the situation.

The other two boys were nowhere to be seen, but the emergency services later found the remains in the adjacent woodland.

The experience broke him, shattering his confidence and sending him into a downward spiral of anxiety and depression.

But with the help of his colleagues, family and professional support he did climb back into the cab.

Gone were the hi-speed, intercity services, and instead he made his living behind the controls of freight trains.

The slower pace suited him now.

He knew his new limitations.

HE'D STARTED his shift very early that morning, up before dawn. He had always liked the early mornings, particularly at this time of year, when the sun was up and the birds singing.

It felt good to be beating the rest of the day - the crowds, the traffic, most of the rest of society.

The peace this morning had however been the quiet before the storm.

His job was to pick up and pull a thirty wagon train from Westgate, a freight depot to the west of London, to the south western port city of Bristol, where it would be loaded onto a ship bound for the Republic of Ireland.

He'd moved out of the train depot shortly after three am, easing the train out of the sidings area, towards the main line. It was too early for the hi-speed services, and the only other traffic was freight trains like his, or empty locomotives being moved into position for the start of the daytime services.

He saw the body up ahead, sprawled out across the tracks.

'Dear God,' he muttered, squinting into the morning sun as he applied the emergency brakes. His heart jackhammered as his train, travelling at a mercifully slow speed this time, jerked to a dead stop.

Rodney gazed out of the front window at the body, panic and horror rising.

It was happening again.

'Hello,' he said, radioing through to the control station. 'Engine 5421.'

'Hello 5421,' the reply came back almost instantly.

Rodney tried to steady his breath. 'I'm calling to report a body on the line. Just out of Westgate Depot.'

'Can you provide any further details? Is the individual deceased?'

'I don't know,' Rodney admitted. 'I'm still in my cab.' He looked out again at the scene. 'But there's no movement. I guess they could...they could be asleep.'

*Maybe that's what it was - someone, maybe drunk or drugged up, had fallen asleep on the line.*

*But how likely was that?*

'Shall I stay in the cab?'

'Yes,' came back the definitive reply. 'Please stay where you are, we don't want any more tragedies this morning.'

'Okay,' Rodney said, relieved but still feeling uncomfortable with his role of mere observer.

'I'll inform emergency services,' the controller explained. 'We should have someone with you in a matter of minutes.'

As the call ended, Rodney placed his head in his hands and began to sob.

# 2

*Previous Saturday evening*

Cullen arrived at Acorn House, the residential care home on the rural outskirts of Wigan, where his childhood friend Philip resided, just after six o'clock on Saturday evening. His wife Sarah had offered to accompany him and her brother Philip en route to the rugby match, but Cullen had declined.

He wanted this to be like the old times.

Just him and Phil. Pint in hand and a great game to watch.

But as he gazed at his mid-forties self in the rear view mirror, he began to regret his decision.

It would never be like the old times.

Those days were long gone.

Cullen and Philip had met as children on the rugby pitch, and been good friends ever since. They'd grown up and grown older together. Philip had introduced Cullen to Sarah, who went on to become the love of his life. As boys and then men they'd played and watched rugby league with a passion, from the terraces of the imposing, iconic Central Park stadium, Wigan, before it had been so cruelly demolished in the 1990's and replaced by a supermarket. And while Cullen cut short his playing career for a life in the police force, Philip turned professional, representing Wigan's rugby league team and Great Britain.

'I just want to make it up to you, mate,' Cullen thought out loud. 'I want to make things right.'

He hadn't dealt well with Philip's diagnosis of early onset dementia. Not well at all. In the early stages, he was there for his friend, but as Philip's condition deteriorated at an alarming rate, Cullen fled in fear.

Fear that his friend's fate could befall him too, given the emerging evidence of how the great collisions on the rugby field take their toll on the brain.

Fear also that a genetic weakness might affect his wife, Sarah.

Cullen shook off his growing misgivings and exited the vehicle with newly found purpose. This was going to be a successful evening. The start of a new beginning, where he would be here for his friend.

He buzzed through to reception and was met by one of the head nurses that he recognised from his previous visit, just a few days ago.

'It's lovely to see you again,' she smiled.

'Thank you.'

'Philip has been really looking forward to you coming,' she said, as Cullen followed her up the stairs.

'Really?'

'Oh yes, you can tell, he's been excited all afternoon, ever since we told him you were coming.'

'That's...great,' he said, surprised and also a little sceptical that the staff could deduce such a thing from a man who rarely spoke and whose face seemed so devoid of emotion.

They moved through a set of double doors into the corridor. 'So you're going to the rugby match?' she asked over her shoulder.

'Yes, Wigan against St. Helens.'

'My husband is going,' she smiled. 'Massive Saints fan.'

The Wigan and Saints derby, between two proud towns just miles apart, was always a passionate, if generally good-natured, affair.

'My commiserations,' Cullen joked.

She laughed. 'I'm sure it will be a great game, whoever wins.'

'I hope so.'

'Seriously though,' she said, 'it's a lovely thing you've done. I'm sure Philip will really benefit from it.'

'Hopefully.'

Cullen had arranged the trip to the match at the last minute, through a local dementia charity. The event included not only a top price ticket to the game, but also an after-match reception where you could meet players, past and present.

Sarah had been reticent about the idea, given the sporadic bouts of aggression that Philip had been displaying recently. But Cullen had persuaded her that it would be okay.

'Philip's waiting in the lounge,' she explained. 'He's all ready to go.'

They emerged into the lounge area, a large room that was designed to look as homely as possible, with its comfy sofas, welcoming fireplace and television. The room was quiet at this relatively late hour, with Philip being only one of three people there. He was sitting in the corner, perched on the edge of the seat, but didn't look at Paul as he approached with the nurse.

A familiar feeling of trepidation washed over Cullen as he pulled across a chair.

'Hey, mate, how are you doing?'

Philip looked up and to Cullen's surprise, smiled.

'You look well,' Cullen said, buzzing inside from the unexpectedly positive reaction. 'Are you ready to go to the game?'

Philip seemed to nod.

Cullen looked up at the nurse. 'What's the best way of doing this?'

'Slowly,' she replied. 'It's the only way.'

THE NURSE HAD BEEN RIGHT. Even making use of the lift, the journey from the lounge to Cullen's car took fifteen minutes. Philip's walking shuffle was glacially slow. Cullen was thankful for the two extra staff members who were on hand for support, given his inexperience at assisting his friend.

'He should be fine, but you just need to keep an eye on him,' the lead nurse advised as they crossed the carpark. 'If there's uneven ground, or crowds, you need to be mindful that he doesn't fall.'

'I will,' Cullen said, conscious that Philip was still quite a man-mountain, and might prove difficult for even him to support if he got too unsteady.

'The people at the event will be there to help you too,' the nurse said. 'They're very experienced, and are well trained health professionals. Quite a few of our residents have been to the rugby events over the years.'

'That's good to know.'

'But if anything happens, just call us on our emergency number. We have transport that can come and collect.'

Cullen examined the card that she handed to him. 'Also good to know.' He slipped it into his pocket. 'Hopefully I won't be needing it.'

'I'm sure it will all be fine,' she said.

Carefully, they helped Philip into the front passenger seat and buckled the seat belt.

'I hope you have a lovely time, Philip,' she said. 'I can't bring myself to wish Wigan good luck,' she smiled at Cullen, 'but I hope it's a great game.'

Cullen said his goodbyes and pulled out onto the main road. As he accelerated through the junction, Philip sitting by his side, he realised (with some guilt) that this was the first time he had been alone with his friend for years.

'It's been too long,' Cullen said to Philip, who was sitting bolt upright, staring ahead. 'I'm sorry, it's my fault, totally. I should have been there for you.'

Cullen glanced across, but there was no reaction from Philip.

But that wasn't to say that he couldn't understand.

*Who really knew?*

On Sarah's suggestion, he would talk to his friend as if he could understand every single word.

'I'm going to make it up to you,' Cullen continued. 'Starting from tonight.'

Cullen turned his attention back to the road as they approached a roundabout. He was so focussed on negotiating the right hand exit that he didn't fully hear the words that Philip uttered.

'What was that, mate?' he asked, as they were back in the normal traffic flow.

But Philip wasn't going to say any more for now.

# 3

*Saturday evening*

THE TRAFFIC SLOWED as they neared the stadium, but they were relatively early, and made good time to the carpark, where they had priority parking right by the stadium entrance.

'You recognise this place?' Cullen said, as he cut the engine and gazed out at the ground. 'Not bad. But it will never be like Central Park, eh?'

He thought Philip gave a small shake of the head, but it might have been his imagination.

Without the support of the Acorn House staff, the journey from car to the special visitors' entrance was nerve-wracking. Cullen linked arms with Philip, and moved slowly and deliberately across the thankfully-smooth tarmac. Once inside, they were directed to an upper lounge via a lift, and welcomed by one the dementia charity team members.

And when it was time for the game, they - along with the

other attendees - were helped to their plush seats in the main stand.

The atmosphere was electric. A capacity crowd, in full voice, welcomed the teams of Wigan and St. Helens onto the pitch. Cullen wondered if the event might prove too much for Philip, surely now so used to the quiet, cosseted environment of his care home. But his smiling friend, although still voiceless, was quite obviously enjoying it as the game kicked off with a series of thunderous, bone-crunching hits.

At half time, Wigan were 12-20 down to an impressive St. Helens side. And by the full time whistle, Saints had extended their lead to twenty points. The 16-36 scoreline was a disappointment, but Cullen couldn't complain about the entertainment value and effort on display.

Following the match, they returned to the lounge where they met past and present Wigan players, fresh from the on-field battle.

'Hey, you're Philip Sullivan, aren't you?' Stuart Warburton, one of the current Wigan players said with a smile. A talented prop forward, he hadn't featured in the game due to injury. 'I remember watching you from the stands as a young lad,' he enthused, as a delighted Paul Cullen watched on. 'That try in the World Club Challenge, against Sydney, man, that is still the most awesome thing I've ever seen on a rugby field.'

He took both of Philip's hands and clasped them together. 'It's great to meet one of my heroes.'

Philip smiled.

Stuart Warburton said his goodbyes as they moved around the other players. A couple of the past players also recognised Philip, and it warmed Cullen's heart.

He sent some texts to Sarah letting her know how well it was going.

By the time they reached Acorn House at the end of the evening, both men were tired. Philip's eyes were heavy, as he was again helped back into the building by the kindly staff. Safely back in Philip's room, the staff retreated while Cullen sat down next to his friend.

'I hope you enjoyed yourself as much as I did,' Cullen said.

Philip nodded.

'I have to go back to London tomorrow,' Cullen continued. He hadn't been sure whether to mention this to him, but decided to be open, in the way he would have done if Philip had been in the best of health. 'I've got work to attend to, unfortunately. But,' he said, as brightly as possible, 'Sarah will be around, and I'll be back up here as soon as possible.'

He watched his friend, sensing that he wanted to say something.

He gave Philip's shoulder a friendly tap. 'What is it, Phil?'

'Good man,' Philip said. 'Good man.'

For the second time in recent days, Cullen left Acorn House in tears.

But this time, he knew he would be back.

~

CULLEN GOT BACK to Philip's house, where Sarah had been staying for the past few weeks since her move back up to Wigan.

Sarah was in the lounge, her legs tucked under her body as she watched the television from the sofa. She smiled.

'Well that was a big success,' Cullen announced, more in relief than in celebration. He plonked himself down next to

Sarah, who shifted position and placed a loving hand on his back.

'Maybe you *can* save everybody,' she joked, rewarding his good evening's work with a peck on the cheek. 'Sounds like it went well.'

Cullen stretched out and exhaled. 'Thank goodness.'

'So no aggression?' she ventured.

'Not from Phil,' he joked, 'but lots on the pitch. Let's hope he doesn't get any ideas.'

'Don't,' she said. 'I hate to think what might happen if he lashes out at one of the staff the way he did with me.'

Earlier that day, Sarah had revealed how Philip had swung at her during a trip to the supermarket. Fortunately he had missed his target, but if he had connected, it might have been serious. And if he did such a thing in Acorn House, it might spell the end of stay there.

'I'm dreading the meeting next week,' Sarah admitted. Senior staff at Acorn House had called a multi-disciplinary meeting to discuss Philip's increasing aggression, to which Sarah as the main family carer had been invited. The worrying development of his increased sporadic acts of aggression, both towards staff and Sarah, posed a genuine threat to his continued stay at the home. Philip's continued imposing physical stature meant the behaviour was a particular worry. 'I'm so scared that they're going to suggest moving him.'

Cullen hugged her. 'I'm sure that's not going to happen. This evening, the staff seemed very positive about him. And I made a point of telling them how good he had been when we were out.'

'Thanks. I hope you're right. If we do have to find somewhere else, I'll be devastated. I mean, Acorn House is perfect for him. Anywhere else, somewhere that isn't as caring, he might just deteriorate even more quickly.'

'Let's just see what they say next week. I'm sorry I can't be there with you.'

'It's fine,' she said. 'There's nothing you can do - your team needs you too.'

Cullen shrugged. 'I'm sure they can manage.'

'And there's Tony of course.'

'Yes.' His long-term policing partner, DS Tony Beswick, was currently recovering in hospital from a serious heart attack that he had suffered while out shopping for his wife Brenda's birthday present on Oxford Street the previous week. Off duty, he'd been giving chase to a hand-bag thief before collapsing on the pavement. 'That reminds me, I need to text Brenda and see how she's doing.'

'I spoke to her tonight,' Sarah revealed. Despite the age difference, Sarah and Brenda had become good friends because of their husband's working relationship. The two families had holidayed together several times. 'She's doing a lot better now that Tony seems to be out of the woods.'

'That's good.'

'But she did tell me that she definitely wants him to retire.'

Sarah dangled the comment for a response.

Brenda had been saying this for a couple of years now, but hadn't yet broken Tony's resistance. Tony loved his job, and dreaded leaving it behind. 'That's something they need to sort out and decide between themselves,' Cullen stated.

'Very diplomatic. I don't blame you. I just listened to her, didn't offer an opinion one way or the other.'

A year ago Cullen had been persuaded by Brenda to

broach the subject of retirement with Tony over a pint, and it hadn't gone well.

'I'm happy to talk to him about it, if he raises it,' Cullen added. 'I still have nightmares about the last time.'

Tony was the least spiky person he knew, but that chat had been a bit of a low point. The situation with Brenda and Tony reminded Cullen of those times when a passerby tries to intervene in a domestic dispute and then gets beaten up by both parties. It really was the kind of situation where it was highly recommended not to get involved, if you cared about your own well-being.

'Just a warning though, she might mention it to you.'

Cullen nodded. 'I can only hope not.'

# 4

*Sunday morning*

CULLEN LEFT EARLY the next morning, saying an emotional goodbye to Sarah from the platform at Wigan North Western station. As much as he didn't want to leave, he needed to get back down to London, ready for the working week ahead.

'I'd prefer to stay here with you,' he said, as they embraced.

'I'd love that too,' Sarah said. She smiled as she squinted against the sun. 'Until next time.'

The train cruised into view.

'Until next time.'

As the train left the station Cullen sat back, dissatisfied with this new long-distance relationship. And although it was meant to be just temporary, the truth was that he could see Sarah staying up here for as long as Philip was alive. After all, he saw for himself the care his friend needed, and deserved.

And it was only going to get more necessary, as Philip's condition inevitably worsened.

He drummed his fingers against the table, thinking long and hard.

Thoughts that until now he hadn't dared or cared to consider.

Maybe it was time to leave London behind.

Maybe it really was time.

~

BEFORE HEADING BACK to the hotel where he'd chosen to set up base for a couple of weeks, Cullen made his way to the hospital to see his good friend, DS Beswick. Now his condition had stabilised, he'd been moved to a regular cardiovascular rehabilitation ward, which he was sharing with three other male patients.

Cullen was struck by how similar the occupants of the other beds looked to Tony. They were all middle-aged, in their fifties or sixties.

His mind turned again to whether he could have helped his friend to have avoided his fate. Although there hadn't been any clear warning signs, it still played on Cullen's mind that he hadn't tried to get his partner to take better care of himself.

Tony was sitting up, propped up by two pillows. There was an open novel on his lap, bent flat across the spine, but he was just staring straight ahead and didn't seem to notice his friend and colleague approach.

'Tony,' Cullen said brightly. 'Thought I'd swing by to say hello before heading back to the delights of my hotel.'

DS Beswick snapped out of his thoughts. 'Oh, hi Boss,

good to see you,' he said, speaking through something of a haze.

Cullen pulled up the garish, uncomfortably-hard orange plastic seat. 'How are things?'

Beswick shrugged and for a moment Cullen thought that his friend was about to cry.

'Shall I pull across the curtains?' Cullen asked.

He nodded, so Cullen swooshed across the thin blue fabric around the perimeter of the bed. 'Make things a bit more cosy,' he joked.

DS Beswick didn't laugh. He just shook his head sadly. 'I hate this place, Paul, I really do.' He looked right at him. 'I just want to get out of here.'

'I know, mate. I know. I would be the same.'

Beswick shook his head. 'I don't know when I'll be able to go home. Hopefully soon.'

'I'm sure it won't be too long,' Cullen said, sitting back down on the rock hard chair. 'I mean, they need the beds.'

'I don't think I can stand much longer in here.'

Cullen tried again to lighten the mood. 'Is the food that bad?'

This time, to Cullen's relief, he did elicit a smile.

'Actually, the grub is okay. Although I didn't expect much. Last night, they did a nice fish and chips. Didn't think too much of the curry the night before. But actually, it's pretty good. I mean, it's got nothing on Brenda's hotpot, of course...'

'Of course.' His wife Brenda was a fine cook, as Cullen had experienced on several occasions when Sarah and he had been invited round for dinner. Brenda's culinary skills partly explained DS Beswick's rounded stomach - although his weekly pints down at the local pub did play their role. 'How is Brenda coping with it all?' Cullen ventured.

She had taken Tony's heart attack hard, and last week had been struggling to come to terms with what had happened. But given what Sarah had said, maybe things were looking up.

'The night out at Cats helped,' Beswick replied. 'Thanks so much for doing that - I really appreciate it.'

'Absolutely no problem,' Cullen replied. He had put aside his hatred of musical theatre to accompany Brenda to the performance which Tony had arranged as his wife's birthday treat. 'You know, I almost enjoyed myself.'

Another welcome smile. 'Liar.'

'Okay, I didn't really enjoy myself, but I didn't hate it as much as I thought I would. Maybe I'm going soft.'

Beswick laughed. 'You're softer than you like to admit, Boss.'

'Maybe.'

Tony frowned, like he had just been reminded of something uncomfortable. He stared at the end of the bed, looking troubled.

'You okay, Tony?'

He shook his head slowly and looked back at Cullen. 'Not really,' he admitted, his eyes pooled with tears.

Cullen wanted to place a hand on him, but resisted - he wasn't really that kind of guy, and Tony definitely wasn't. 'What's up? Apart from the obvious.'

Tony pinched the tears away. 'It's over, Paul. My career as a police officer is over.'

~

CULLEN TOOK IN THE WORDS, saw the look on his colleague's face. He'd been expecting this moment for a couple of years now, when retirement was first brought up as a possibility. But it still saddened him to know that they had now reached this point.

'I had a long chat with Brenda last night,' Tony revealed. 'A real heart to heart. We talked things through, and overnight I've come to a decision. It's the right decision.'

He didn't look too convinced.

'You're sure about this?' Cullen felt he needed to say. After all, it was still a very emotional time for Tony and Brenda, and maybe not the best time to be making decisions of that magnitude.

'Of course I'm not sure,' he joked. 'I love my job. Always have. Ever since that first day, starting in the Met, it's been a dream, and in many ways I don't want it to end. But everything comes to an end eventually.'

Cullen nodded at Tony's uncharacteristically poignant statement. 'Very philosophical. You certainly don't owe the force, or the people of London, anything. You're the best cop I've had the pleasure of knowing.'

'I just wish I could have caught him,' Tony said.

'Who?'

'The thief!' he said, surprised that it needed any explanation.

Cullen shrugged, realising that Tony was referring to the bag-snatching guy who Beswick had chased along Oxford Street last week, before coming to a near-fatal stop as his heart gave way. 'You win some, you lose some,' was all he could manage.

'Too true,' Beswick agreed. 'Too...true...'

'The most important thing is that you're okay. You really wouldn't want to have taken your last breath outside John Lewis...'

'No...that's right...' he said, distracted.

Cullen could sense that his colleague wanted to say something else, so he waited until the void was filled.

'I'm scared, Paul,' Tony said finally, fixing him with a look that asked for help.

'Scared about dying?'

He shook his head. 'Scared about leaving the force. It's been my life for over thirty years. I can hardly remember anything else. I'm scared of what might happen to me when I walk away. Will I be the same person?'

This time Cullen did chance a comforting hand on his friend's shoulder. 'I understand. I'm sure I'll be the same, when my time comes. Actually, I'll probably be even worse. But the time after, it will be amazing for you. Just think of all those cruises Brenda is probably already booking you both on.'

He chuckled. 'You're not wrong there.' He twisted and reached across for a holiday brochure that had been lying on the bedside cabinet. 'She left this with me, and has circled a few trips. Said I've got first choice though.'

'There you go then,' Cullen said, flicking through the brochure at the pictures of ocean liners and exotic locations. 'The world is your oyster, as they say.'

'Yeah, never really understood that saying.'

'Me neither. But you get the point.' He handed him back the brochure. 'You're going to have the best time. Yes, you'll miss your amazing colleagues,' he smiled, 'but I'm sure you'll survive.'

Tony had brightened. 'And I can always come over to visit.'

'HQ. Yes, sure. You're always welcome. We'll roll out the red carpet.'

'Put on a spread?'

'Definitely. Pork pies, peanuts and cake.'

'I'll be there.'

'When you're not at sea...'

'Yes.'

Cullen looked again at his friend, in this unnatural, sterile environment, still seeming somewhat vulnerable and emotional. 'You don't owe the force anything,' Cullen repeated.

Beswick nodded.

'I could save this for your leaving do,' Cullen continued, 'but now seems like a good time to say how much I've valued your presence during the past few years. I wouldn't be in the position I'm in now without your guidance and support.'

They'd been partners since day one, and Tony had been an unfailing mentor and champion of Paul's as Cullen had risen through the ranks of the British Transport Police. There had never been a second of jealously of Cullen's rocket-like rise, and as far as Paul was concerned the guy was second to none.

'Nonsense,' Beswick dismissed. 'You were heading for the stars, Boss.'

Cullen shook his head. 'I was nearly on the next train back to Wigan. You were the one person who made the difference, helped me to settle in, not just to the job, but to a new place.'

Tony had been a huge help during those initial few months in the capital, when Cullen had genuinely fought severe second-thoughts about his move down south.

Beswick looked genuinely touched, his face even flushing slightly. He shifted in his bed. 'Well, what can I say?'

'You don't need to say anything. But promise me one thing.'

'Sure.'

'You'll invite us around regularly to experience the wonders of Brenda's cooking.'

'Oh, yes, definitely.'

# 5

*Sunday afternoon*

'What the hell are they doing here?' Shazney Powell asked, looking across the room at the group of men huddled around a table in the corner. The Sunday afternoon event was meant to have been a place for Tyrone Green's family and friends to get together and remember him. But they were neither friends or family.

*They were laughing and joking!*

Her father Malcolm put a protective arm around her. 'It's okay, Angel, they're here for Tyrone.'

'I didn't see them at the funeral last week,' she shot back. 'They're here for the free food and drink.'

She looked across again at the group and the ringleader, a guy called Carlton, whom she particularly disliked, caught her gaze as he swigged from a bottle.

'Let's go over and see some of the others,' her father said, keen to direct her attention somewhere else.

'I need to go to the bathroom,' she replied, slipping out of his embrace and heading across what was normally a dance floor.

Shazney used the facilities and exited the cubicle, taking the time while she washed her hands to try and calm down a little.

All these people, friends and relatives, they didn't know the truth about what had led to Tyrone's violent death.

*That man, did he assault you?*

She and Tyrone had been in the middle of a heated discussion. He hadn't told her that their day out in Central London would also involve a stop-off to pick up drugs from a go-between at Euston Station.

'Tyrone, please, you promised you were going to stop all this. Just for today, leave it,' she had pleaded with him in the tube carriage. 'You and me, we can have a lovely day, without all this.'

He had promised her time and again that he would move away from dealing and supplying and find a proper job.

'I can't babe, I can't,' he had whispered into her ear. 'One day, I will, but not today.'

She thought that she would succeed in taming him where others, including her best friend Rochelle, had failed. But in recent weeks she'd come to the painful realisation that she had been fooling herself.

'So you're still going to do it?' she had said, boiling with rage as he refused to abort his drugs mission. She had shrugged off his attempt to placate her with inappropriate, intimate physical contact.

'Babe...'

'Go to hell, Tyrone,' she spat, as the train stopped at the station and the doors slid open.

'I'm sorry,' he had said, with one last look.

And with that, Tyrone was gone.

'That man, did he assault you?' the towering figure of a man had asked, appearing as if from nowhere.

'Yeah, he did.'

It was a split second reaction, not even a decision, when the question was asked. The guy had appeared at the apex of her anger, and she didn't think at all about the implications of her response.

'Don't worry, he won't get away with it.'

She'd regretted her actions immediately, but it was too late.

Events were set in motion.

'Paul Cullen, British Transport Police. Call me.' She looked at the card he had given her, wondering what on earth she had done.

She'd hurried as fast as she could off the train and out of the underground station, pushing past slow-moving passengers, but had lost sight of the plain clothes officer. Emerging onto the concourse, she had expected to see Tyrone detained by the police. But instead, through the entrance, she saw her boyfriend take flight and the officer in pursuit.

She had never been a great runner, but she ran for her life after them.

'Tyrone!'

Chest tightening with exertion, she'd pushed forward with increasing difficulty as, some distance up ahead, Tyrone fled across the busy main road that ran past the front of the station.

Horns blared out their warning and tyres screeched in futile evasive manoeuvres.

Tyrone had been hit by a bus.

'Nooooo!'

She had seen his body skim along the road, straight into the path of a lorry.

'Tyrone! T-y-r-o-n-e!'

Acid and terror rising, Shazney had come to a sudden stop next to the horrific scene where her boyfriend lay dead in the arms of the police officer. Tyrone's body had been twisted and crushed by the impact with the heavy vehicle, and his eyes stared out widely.

'You've killed him!' she had screamed at the officer as thick, heavy tears clouded her vision. 'You've killed my boyfriend!'

Except that - even then - she knew that it wasn't true.

And then she back in the present, in the washroom, alone. A present that was no longer normal. No longer happy. It was a warped version of itself, polluted forever by that awful event.

'I killed him,' she said into the bathroom mirror, daring her reflection to offer any defence. 'I killed Tyrone.'

~

SHAZNEY EMERGED FROM THE BATHROOM, having tried to hide the fact that she'd been tearful, and kept her head low as she passed by the mourners.

'It's so weird,' a voice said from her left. 'Seeing the place like this.'

It was Harmony, Shazney's boss at the beauty salon where she worked. The two hugged, having not had the chance at the service, and Harmony offered her a sad, sympathetic smile.

Harmony wasn't only Shazney's boss, she was also a

mentor, being several years older than the twenty year old and now a successful business woman. Harmony, along with her cousin Harvey, offered a model of how to not only survive in the challenging environment in which they lived, but to thrive.

'It's normally so throbbing with life in here, isn't it?' Harmony continued, looking around. 'So full of laughter and lots of good times. But not today.'

'It seems like such a different place,' Shazney agreed.

Harmony's dad owned the club, and being a friend of the family in their close knit community, had offered it for free as a venue for the get together.

'I'm surprised they're here,' Harmony said disdainfully, giving a subtle gesture towards Carlton and his friends, still laughing in the corner. 'If you ask me, they're the cause of all this. We spent years trying to extract Tyrone from those people. But we just couldn't do it.'

'I know you did.'

Tyrone had been a part of the drug-fuelled gang scene that had flourished across London. Targeted and recruited from an early age by gang leaders, like so many other young boys in the neighbourhood, he'd been immersed and enveloped by the culture of violence and crime that seemed all too normal in this part of the capital. He began to use his absent, imprisoned father's surname of "Edwards" and worked his way up the hierarchy, gaining respect through fear.

The truth was, despite the efforts of Harmony and the others, Tyrone seemed to want that life. It was all he knew.

'I saw your dad talking with Carlton,' Harmony revealed. 'He was over there, just now, with the group.'

'Oh.'

'Maybe he was asking them what they were doing here,' Harmony offered, seeing Shazney's disquiet.

'Maybe.' Shazney was thinking through the possible reasons why her dad would want to talk to Carlton and his band of idiots. Surely there was nothing good to come out of engaging with that man, that violence-loving gangster, who had ensured that Tyrone remained firmly entwined in his world - despite Shazney's best efforts at persuading him to cut himself free. 'I expect he was just being polite.'

Harmony shook her head, looking over at them again. 'They know that no-one wants them here. That's why they've come.'

'Probably.'

'Well I'd go over there myself and tell them they're not welcome...'

'But it would be just what they're hoping for,' Harvey said, appearing at her shoulder, 'wouldn't it, cuz?'

'Exactly,' Harmony said.

'I'm really sorry about Tyrone,' Harvey turned to Shazney. 'I can't pretend we were the best of friends, but I'll remember the good times at school, before things changed.'

Shazney nodded. Both Harvey and Harmony had warned her off dating Tyrone when they first became an item, but Shazney was strong willed and had resisted their advice.

'And just remember,' Harvey said. 'Tyrone was a victim. We were just schoolboys when it all started. The only difference is that some of us managed to get out, while others didn't.'

Harvey had once been on the same path, up to his neck in criminality. But the articulate yet wayward young man had managed to turn his life around through a young offenders' education programme at a local college. And now he was completing a degree in design at North London University.

'You think Carlton is a victim too?' Harmony said, incredulously, watching as the guy slapped down hard on the table with an inappropriately loud laugh.

'Even Carlton, cuz, even Carlton.'

# 6

*Monday morning*

CULLEN ARRIVED at Westgate freight yard just after eight on Monday morning, having come straight from the hotel. He had been just about to leave for Headquarters when the call came through about the body find, at the rail depot to the west of the city. Although only limited details had been relayed to him, it was clear the situation was in his remit.

'Paul, good to see you again, so soon. Well, kind of,' Detective Inspector Marianne McGuire said, as she approached.

Cullen nodded. 'Good to see you too, Marianne.'

It was always a pleasure to see DI McGuire, the talented Irish officer from the London regional branch of the British Transport Police. Although their meeting on the job could ever only mean one thing - that a serious crime had been committed. The regional branch dealt with lower level crimes across the capital's transport network, while Cullen's Major and Serious Organised Crime department picked up the worst offences that happened across the country - murder, serious sexual crimes, organised criminal activities.

At the nexus was where their paths crossed - the regional team were most often the first on scene, even for cases that were sooner or later passed over to Cullen and his colleagues. Sometimes the regional and national teams worked together, as had happened the previous week when Marianne and Cullen had investigated the death of a young woman who had fallen onto the tracks at Angel tube station.

'The body was found in the early hours of this morning,' DI McGuire explained as they walked side by side across the siding area towards the site of police activity. Old abandoned trains and carriages littered the tracks, like toys abandoned by a toddler.

'By a train driver?' Cullen asked, to confirm the brief details that he'd been told over the phone.

'By a driver, yes. The guy's over there,' she said, gesturing towards a building on the left. 'He's still pretty shaken up by it all. Seems it's triggered some past trauma.'

'Previous fatality incident?' Cullen had seen it many times before, the lasting legacy of being involved in the death of people on the tracks. Drivers were prepared for these things as much possible, and received comprehensive post-incident care from occupational health team, but sometimes nothing would be enough.

'Yes. Children. Four of them.'

Cullen puffed out his cheeks at the thought of it. He had nothing but sympathy for those trying to cope with meeting death on the tracks. Even as an experienced, hardened Detective Chief Inspector, Cullen struggled sometimes to deal with the sights, sounds and smells to which his job exposed him.

'Has the body been identified?' Cullen said, as they

reached the trackside where the body still lay, protected within a white tent. Scene of crime officers were busying themselves.

'Not yet,' Marianne replied. 'He's a white male, late thirties. No distinguishing features. The guy had no ID on his person - no wallet, no phone. Looked like he's dressed in lounge-wear, as if he was ready for bed, or a late night movie. He was wearing trainers, but no socks.'

'Strange. Definitely not dressed for a night-time walkabout.'

'No,' she agreed. 'We've put a call out for missing persons, see if anyone has reported anything. Doing some digging too through various other avenues, see if we can get the name quickly.'

As they both knew, the first few hours after a murder were often the most crucial. If traction could be gained, before the trail went cold, a case could be solved relatively quickly. But it really needed that early breakthrough of information to push forward the investigation.

'Maybe he was sleepwalking?' Cullen threw out there.

'You want to see the body?' Marianne asked, deflecting the question with one of her own.

'It's okay,' Cullen said. 'I don't want to get in the way of your investigation.'

'Your investigation,' she corrected.

'Are you sure?'

She nodded. 'One hundred percent certain.'

'So you're certain there was foul play?' Cullen asked.

'The man had died sometime before being discovered,'

Marianne replied. That's pretty obvious. 'Not only that, but it's clear that the body was placed on the tracks - it definitely wasn't the scene of death.'

Cullen took that in. 'There are clear tracks?'

Marianne nodded. 'Whoever did this, didn't make much effort to cover their tracks. There are footprints leading up to the trackside, in the dirt. And the stones in between the tracks strongly suggest the body was dragged from the location of the footprints.'

'Any obvious cause of death?'

'From an initial assessment, blunt force trauma to the head. But I'm just waiting for an update on that.'

Cullen thought about the perpetrator dragging the body to its trackside resting place. 'CCTV?' he asked, looking around to spot the cameras. There were some, but the coverage probably wouldn't be great, as the cameras were an old type and over in the far corner, meaning their resolution would leave a lot to be desired, particularly in the dark.

'Anthony Braddock is on the case,' Marianne added. 'I'm just waiting to hear back.'

Cullen nodded. Anthony Braddock, head of the National Railways CCTV Hub, would pull out all the stops to help. Cullen had owed many a breakthrough to that man's ability to quickly and effectively source footage from across the country's network of trackside and station cameras.

If anyone could identify something interesting from the footage, it would be Anthony.

'There is something else which seems to be significant,' Marianne revealed.

'Go on...'

'As I said, the guy didn't have any ID on his person. But we did find something in his trouser pocket. A handwritten note.'

'Oh?'

'It said: "Soon everyone will know what you really are!".'

'Very interesting,' Cullen replied. 'A message from the killer, maybe.'

'Maybe.'

'Very interesting,' Cullen repeated, thinking more about the message. If it was from the person who had killed this man, it was pretty bold to leave it on the body, ready for the police to find.

'I take it you'd like to speak to the driver?' Marianne asked, interrupting Cullen's thoughts.

'That would be great.'

It wasn't that Cullen didn't trust the officers already on scene to have already got the necessary information from this key witness. It was that when leading an investigation, Cullen placed great importance on ensuring he had that personal, face-to-face connection with each and every person involved, even if it was just that one initial meeting, however brief. It could make a huge difference to the investigation, meeting the key actors face-to-face. Sometimes it had led to the identification of a possible suspect, when before they had gone under the radar. More often, it had resulted in vital information being divulged by people to him. Countless times he'd been contacted by people after meeting them, with new revelations about a case that had taken investigations forward in a way that otherwise would not have been considered.

'Like I said, he's over there, in the workers' office,' Marianne explained. 'You okay to go there on your own? I'll just see how the guys are doing with the body.'

'Fine. And I will take a look at the body, right after this.'

He strode across the yard towards the office, wondering what this could yield. He was beckoned in after a polite knock on the door.

The office was small and untidy, with papers over most of the surfaces. A man approached and introduced himself as the manager of the site. He directed him towards an adjoining room where the driver was sitting, cradling a hot mug of tea.

'Detective Chief Inspector Paul Cullen, British Transport Police,' Cullen said, holding out a hand. The driver smiled sadly and Cullen could see the anxiety radiating from him.

'You got all you need?' Marianne asked, as Cullen exited the office, following his discussion with the train driver and a quick look at the body.

'I think so,' he replied, crunching across the gravel that lay by the track-side. He stopped just a little way from the building, looking over towards the white scene of crime tent. 'Your officers have already got all the necessary information,' he said. 'There's not much more to the story.'

'What are you thinking?' Marianne asked, as Cullen continued to look over at the activity around the tent.

'I'm thinking that the poor guy in there is going to need some careful support,' he said, referring to the driver. 'He really is in a bad way - it's triggered very painful memories. He was telling me about what happened with those kids.' Cullen shook his head. 'It's something that he's obviously never got over, which isn't a surprise. I don't expect you ever do.'

'Well we know all about that, don't we?' Marianne replied.

Cullen nodded. It was true. All sections of the police saw horrific sights during their career, and it was no different in the British Transport Police. To a large extent, Cullen had become hardened to the scenes of horror that he frequently encountered, but it had taken some time to get to that point. Those first few call outs to deaths on the tracks were still the most vivid in his mind - images that would stay with him like unwelcome house visitors. 'At least we know what we're getting ourselves in to. He just signed up to drive a train.'

'Maybe,' she said. 'I'm not sure I knew exactly what I was getting myself into, when I joined the force.'

Cullen turned to his colleague, detecting a rare note of self-doubt from the usually confident and assured DI McGuire. 'But you'd do it again, if you could?'

Marianne nodded. 'Without a shadow of a doubt.'

'Good to hear it,' he said. 'You're a good officer, and we need all the good officers we've got.'

'How's DI Beswick?' she asked, correctly interpreting Cullen's thought process.

'Doing okay,' he said. 'Out of the woods I think, in terms of his heart. Although he has to be careful of course. He's decided to retire.'

'Right,' she said. 'So that's why you're all melancholic.'

Cullen laughed at her perceptiveness. 'I'll miss the guy, that's for certain.'

'You'll need a new partner.'

'Looks like I've got one,' he joked, patting her on the back. 'Tony actually suggested it - said you're a fine officer and worthy replacement for him.'

Marianne smiled. 'I always thought he was a good judge of character.'

# 7

*Monday morning*

CULLEN LEFT Marianne to continue with the on-scene investigations and headed over to the British Transport Police Headquarters, located in Camden Town, North London.

Home to the British Transport Police's Central Division, which had a national remit to prevent and investigate crimes across the rail network, it was the base for the National Serious and Organised Crime department, which Cullen headed up. The building was a 1960's concrete monstrosity, but its ugly exterior hid the beauty of the work within it, where his team investigated serious crimes on the transport network across the country. The investigative activities of the British Transport Police was largely out of the public view - many wouldn't even know of its existence. But it was a depressingly busy area of policing, solving cases of murder, sexual assault, and gang-related criminality nationwide.

Cullen's team were mirrored by a team up in Leeds, who

dealt predominately with cases in the North and Midlands. Meanwhile he focussed on London, which was busy enough on its own, the South East, and South West of England. They worked closely with their regional colleagues, such as DI McGuire, who focussed mainly on the less serious end of the criminal spectrum.

Cullen entered the main investigation room, a large open plan office filled with workstations. He did a round of hellos among his team, checking that everyone was alright and there was nothing else urgent that had come in that morning. There had been a gang-related fight the previous evening on a train in East London, a serious sex attack on a lady on a bus in Plymouth, and Detective Sergeant Alex Summers, his youngest and most promising officer, was just taking details about a hate crime incident in Brighton.

Just the usual start to the working week.

Cullen headed into his office, calling in his colleague, DI Danny Lomax, as he booted up his computer.

'Danny, I'd like you to work with me on something that's happened this morning,' he said.

Danny was downstairs in the cafeteria. 'I'll be right up, Boss,' he said in his broad Essex accent. A key member of the team, Danny was a trusted officer who had been at Headquarters for just over five years.

'I'll explain when you get up,' Cullen said. 'Oh, and mine's a latte.'

'Sure thing.'

'Here you go,' DI Lomax said, handing Cullen the latte. He slid down in the seat beside the small, round meeting table that nestled in the corner of Cullen's office. 'Nice weekend?'

'Really nice,' Cullen replied. 'Apart from the rugby result.'

'I saw that,' DI Lomax said. 'Bad luck.'

Cullen was impressed that Danny had actually taken enough interest to know the result - he wasn't a fan of the oval ball game, being a huge West Ham United football fan.

'I see West Ham won again,' Cullen noted. 'Aren't you top five now?'

Cullen had about as much interest in football as Danny had in rugby league, but he kept abreast of developments in the Premier League - it helped with team banter among a cohort of football-loving cops.

'Top four,' Danny corrected proudly. 'Let's hope it lasts - I can't believe it really. We've got Liverpool next week,' he said ominously.

'I bet DI Gasnier is happy,' Cullen noted. The Met officer whom he had got to know since his arrival in the capital was also a huge West Ham fan.

'Dead right he is. So, Boss, what's happening then, I hear you were called out early this morning.'

Cullen explained the situation, while Danny worked his way through a flapjack, dropping crumbs onto the office floor.

'Sounds like an interesting one,' Danny noted, popping the last bit of flapjack into his mouth just in time for the end of Cullen's tale.

'I hoped you'd think so,' Cullen said.

'Who was there from London branch?' Danny asked.

'Marianne,' Cullen replied, knowing exactly what his colleague was thinking.

DI Lomax and Marianne had been an item, before a painful split last year. They had managed to avoid one another since the break up, despite Cullen's attempts to bring them to some kind of rapprochement.

'Right,' Danny said, perturbed.

'It might be good for you two to work together,' Cullen tried. He really didn't like to see two of his favourite people suffering, and it had seemed clear that deep down both Marianne and Danny wanted to repair their damaged relationship.

'Maybe,' Danny replied. 'I'll do some digging,' he said, following a pregnant pause, 'see whether we can come up with anything. I'll liaise with London branch, make sure I don't tread on any toes.'

Cullen was actually quite surprised by his colleague's positive attitude to working with his ex. 'Good, thanks Danny.'

Alone again in the office, Cullen thought about Sarah and Philip, and the meeting on Wednesday.

He wished he could be there to support them.

But was he really willing to give up his career?

He was still lost in thought when the internal call came through.

It was Rose, the Executive Personal Assistant.

'Sir, DS Maggie Ferguson would like to see you.'

'Now?'

'Yes, immediately, if possible.'

# 8

*Monday morning*

'DO COME IN.'

Cullen entered Detective Superintendent Maggie Ferguson's office. His formidable boss, with a strong Glaswegian accent and even stronger sense of duty, never failed to intimidate even the hardest of officers. Her fierce reputation, forged during her incredibly successful time with Police Scotland, had been well deserved. She had taken on police corruption north of the border, rooting out officers who had operated on both sides of the law.

'Nice morning, isn't it?' Maggie Ferguson noted, as she stood staring out of the full height windows, her hands clasped behind her back like a headteacher of old.

'Lovely,' Cullen replied. And it was a brilliant day. Not a day for the office, that was for certain.

She turned and Cullen knew from that first look that something was wrong.

'Please, do take a seat,' she said.

He duly complied and they faced one another. Maggie Ferguson actually looked uncomfortable - not a sight he had seen before - and it made him very nervous.

'So, you wanted to see me?'

'Yes,' she said. 'I wanted to talk to you about Operational Archangel.'

'Okay...'

Operational Archangel had been the British Transport Police's flagship programme over the past three months, with Cullen as its lead. Targeting sexual crimes on London's transport network, it had involved a huge resource and commitment from the force.

'How do you feel about the way things have gone?' she asked.

The Operation had not been without its critics, particularly in recent weeks, but overall it had been well received by the press and had received strong support from the main stakeholders across London. Many perpetrators had been apprehended, and with each arrest the tube and buses were that bit safer. It also sought to send out a message to others out there, thinking of doing similar, that the police would pursue them relentlessly.

'I'm incredibly proud of what we've done, and what we've achieved,' was Cullen's honest and heartfelt reply.

She nodded and fixed him with a stare. 'You should be proud. You all should. Archangel was good for us, and good for Londoners.'

Her choice of tense was not lost on Cullen.

*Was good?*

'You can't be ending the Operation?'

'I'm sorry, Paul.'

'BUT IT'S BEEN SUCH a success...I was under the impression that we would be able to run with it, at least for another few months,' he said. 'You said, just a few weeks ago...'

'The shifting sands of politics,' Maggie Ferguson smiled tightly.

'I don't understand.'

'The Mayor is not supporting us anymore.'

'What?' The Mayor had been one of the operation's biggest supporters, and its driving force in the early days when they had desperately needed that high level political commitment.

'He is still supportive personally, of course, of what Archangel aimed to do, and he is grateful for our achievements. But it's become, how should I say it, increasingly politically difficult for him.'

'This is because of the election?'

'Yes,' she said. 'The Mayor's Office has in the past few weeks come to see Archangel as a problem rather than a solution.'

Cullen shook his head.

'You've seen the criticism that the Mayor has been receiving from the press this month,' she continued. 'I mean, the London Daily Post, they're a dog with a bone on this.'

The London Daily Post, the capital's free daily newspaper, often took an antagonistic stance against the police and political establishment.

'The Post are desperate to up their circulation with any campaign they can think of. It wasn't long ago that they were campaigning for something just like Archangel to be introduced.'

'I know, Paul, I know. But the Mayor's opponents have weaponised Archangel, and that's when things get very difficult.'

'Sean Berry?'

'I'm sure that's playing a part,' she admitted.

Sean Berry was currently running a strong second place in the Mayoral race. Once seen as a weak outsider, he had recently landed a few blows on the Mayor, particularly relating to knife crime and sexual violence.

Another shake of Cullen's head.

'Please don't take this personally, Paul,' Maggie advised. 'Or as a sleight to all our good work. It really isn't.'

'Public safety shouldn't be a political football.'

'It's a political decision, most certainly, but one that I'm afraid we've got no chance but to roll with.'

'And Londoners' safety and security suffers,' Cullen replied.

'We have to ensure that doesn't happen,' she said, serious. 'The end of Archangel doesn't mean the end of our mission, to protect and serve all Londoners and visitors to this great city.'

'Of course,' Cullen agreed, trying to fight his profound disappointment. Despite what Maggie said, the death of Archangel would be a real blow, both to the morale of his team and also, he felt, to Londoners.

'I share your disappointment, Paul,' she said. 'But the reality is, that without the support of the Mayor, the operation is dead in the water.'

'I understand.'

'Maybe after the election, if he's re-elected, things may change.'

'Maybe.'

'In the meantime, we need to think more imaginatively about how to build on the great success of Archangel.'

Cullen couldn't really think of how at this moment in time, and it obviously showed on his face.

'I met with the Mayor yesterday,' Maggie Ferguson continued, 'and he wants to see our good work continue. You know he's keen on the use of technology, and also is passionate about engaging the community to solve our biggest challenges.'

'Yes.'

'Well, he wants us to look into MayDay, see what the possibilities are for crime detection and prevention, particularly on the transport network.'

'You mean to collaborate with the makers of it?'

'The Mayor is open to that possibility.'

The force had only in the last few weeks become aware of MayDay, an app that enabled users to alert fellow passengers to incidents of sexual violence. It used technology to communicate with others nearby, who could then come to the victim's aid.

The app had seemed to come from nowhere, hitting the top of the download charts, and the force still didn't know anything about the people behind it. There didn't appear to be an obvious money-making opportunity with the app, but Cullen was convinced that the motive of its creators had to be financial.

'You know my concerns about it,' Cullen said. He'd discussed it with her just last week. 'I'm all for empowering the public, but not vigilantism.'

'We haven't had any negative instances yet though, have we?'

'No,' he conceded. 'But we haven't had any successes either.'

Up until now, no official reports had come through to the police identifying any suspects via use of the app.

'Not that we know about,' she countered. 'We don't know whether there are civilian-led interventions that have gone under the radar. It's also possible that the widespread use of the app is acting as an effective deterrent.'

'I'm still not convinced,' he maintained. 'I suppose time will tell whether it's a help or a hindrance.'

'It's early days,' she agreed. 'Worth thinking about, though, Paul?'

'Well if the Mayor says so.'

'Good. Good,' she said, smiling, choosing to ignore Cullen's less-than-enthusiastic response. 'I'll leave that to you then.'

Cullen made to stand. 'Is that all?'

'Not quite,' she replied, as Cullen rested back on the seat. 'How is everything with you?'

'Err, good,' he said, sideswiped somewhat by the conversation's change of direction.

'The incident with Tyrone Green, you've managed to put that behind you?'

Tyrone Green, also known as Tyrone Edwards. The man whom Cullen had pursued from the tube after suspecting him of sexual assault, only to see him killed in a road traffic collision outside Euston Station.

'Yes,' he lied. 'You know what it's like, in the force, you have to move on.'

In truth, the incident with Tyrone Green was still playing on his mind. Just last night he had dreamed about the chase out of

Euston Station and along towards the main road. He had again watched as the bus had slammed into the young man, sending him skidding across the busy main road and right under the heavy wheels of an articulated lorry. The sights and sounds were all there, and as Cullen knelt down beside the broken boy, it had all seemed so real. And then the screams of Shazney Powell, crashing in like a tidal wave of despair from behind him.

'He's dead. You killed my boyfriend!

'Indeed,' she said slowly, obviously thinking about something. She gazed at Cullen. 'Although I'm not convinced you have moved on.'

Cullen didn't deny it.

'That reporter, Adrian Spencer,' Ferguson continued, 'he's been a bit of a thorn in your side. Gatecrashing the seminar about Archangel, for example.'

Adrian Spencer, an unscrupulous reporter for the new online click-bait newspaper London Lines, had indeed been somewhat of a thorn.

'I can handle him,' Cullen dismissed.

Spencer was using Shazney Powell, the girlfriend of Tyrone Green, to make money. Cullen was determined to extract her from his grip.

Maggie Ferguson mused on that. 'I've been thinking about the meeting you agreed to. I've also been speaking to our comms team. I just don't think it's a good idea, Paul.'

Cullen had agreed to meet with Shazney and Spencer, to discuss Tyrone's death. It was a high risk strategy to engage directly, but Cullen felt confident it would work.

'I think it will help to put out the fire that Spencer is trying to stoke - kill the story,' Cullen replied. 'And more importantly, I think it will help Shazney, both to escape his clutches and to grieve properly.'

'It could go very wrong.'

'Zack Carter from the London Daily Post has agreed to be there too.'

'Will that help?' she asked, unconvinced.

'He's a good journalist.'

'He's a journalist.'

Cullen conceded the point. 'He's young, but he's a match for Spencer. He's also got morals, and will want to see the right thing done by way of us and Shazney. It will disrupt Spencer's plans, and seriously peeve him off in the process.'

Ferguson shook her head slowly.

Cullen didn't really want to ask the question, but he had to. 'Are you saying I can't do it?'

'I'm afraid so, Paul. You need to call it off.'

'You're the boss,' he replied after several beats, a little more curtly than he intended.

'Yes, I am. And often that means making the unpopular, but necessary decisions. You know that, Paul.'

'I do,' he said, already softening. She was probably right, it could have gone wrong. Maybe it was best to ignore Spencer's trolling, and starve him of a story. He'd more than likely slink off under his rock until something else came along to tempt him back into the light.

Hopefully something not involving Cullen or his team.

'Good. Well, I'll let you go now, Paul,' Maggie Ferguson said, satisfied with the outcome of their conversation. 'I don't want to keep you.'

Cullen nodded and made for the door.

'Oh, Paul,' Ferguson said, just before he exited. 'Anything to report on your man on the tracks case? I heard about it this morning. Quite a start to the week.'

'Nothing at the moment,' he admitted, pausing at the

doorway, feeling honoured yet slightly concerned that she expected to see such a rapid breakthrough. 'But give it time.'

He could have gone into things, but he knew Maggie Ferguson wouldn't be concerned about the detail. 'I'm sure we'll get a breakthrough soon enough.'

'On that I have no doubt,' she replied.

# 9

*Monday afternoon*

'WE'VE IDENTIFIED THE VICTIM,' DI Lomax announced, as he entered Cullen's office early that afternoon.

'No way,' Cullen said, amazed at the speed of the success. Even Maggie Ferguson would be impressed.

'A man was reported missing early this morning by his wife,' Danny continued. 'Left the family home late last night, without saying goodbye. He left his wallet, phone, coat in the house and didn't return. Photo matches that of the body found this morning.'

Danny placed a piece of paper on Cullen's desk. 'Michael Gossage,' the detective said.

Cullen took the sheet, which was a profile page from a school website. The man was beaming a broad smile – the photograph was definitely of the man they had found on the tracks that morning.

'He's a school teacher,' Cullen mused, reading down the

information. 'Head of year nine. Taught history at the school for ten years. Thirty five years old, married with one child.'

'By all accounts, a popular and experienced teacher,' Danny said. 'I've been looking at one of those teacher forums, where people can rate teachers, and the comments and ratings are top notch - parents and pupils seem to love him.'

'They're going to be devastated,' Cullen noted, thinking back to a few years ago when a popular female teacher at Amy's school had died of breast cancer. It had really shaken the students, and for Amy, who was already suffering from anxiety, it hit particularly hard.

'They're going to need support, that's for sure,' DI Lomax agreed.

Cullen looked again at Michael's smiling image. On the face of it, he didn't look like the sort of person who had enemies who would seek to do him harm. But Cullen was far too experienced to jump to conclusions.

He thought back to the cryptic note that had been found on his person.

Dark horses and all that.

'Time to speak to his family,' Cullen said. 'You want to take the lead on this?'

'Is...Marianne...?'

'Yes, she'll continue to be involved,' Cullen said.

'Maybe leave it to you, Boss, if you don't mind,' he said. 'I can support from here.'

'No problem.'

Cullen was secretly quite pleased at being given the opportunity to speak with the guy's wife. As DCI his role was of course more strategic, but their team was small enough, and his desire for on-the-ground detective policing strong enough, to warrant his direct involvement.

Plus, there was nothing more helpful to understanding a case than to immerse yourself in it. And that meant getting out from behind your desk.

Sometimes Cullen's insistence on getting involved on the ground frustrated Maggie Ferguson. But she understood that was how he worked best, and that it kept his passion for the job burning brightly.

# 10

*Monday afternoon*

'NICE AREA,' DI McGuire commented, as they alighted the train that afternoon and made their way towards Michael Gossage's home along tree lined streets. They had met en route, at Charing Cross railway station, before traveling east together on the thirty five minute overground train journey to Bexley.

'Very,' he agreed. 'It must be just down there,' he directed towards a side road. The house was half way down the street, its red door resembling a pillar box. Cullen noted the children's drawing stuck on one of the top windows as they approached through the gate.

Poor kid.

Cullen let Marianne knock as they waited for Michael's wife, Jenny, to answer. Back at HQ he had spoken to her briefly on the phone, to check that she would be there.

He'd also taken a call from Anthony Braddock, who

unfortunately hadn't come up with anything to shed light on how Michael's body had been transported to his trackside resting place, or by whom.

As expected, the cover of darkness, and the absence of good quality camera footage, had done its job.

The perpetrator must have known what they were doing.

'Hi,' the woman said, as he answered the door, looking between Cullen and Marianne. 'Police?'

The lady, unsurprisingly, looked washed out. She probably hadn't slept, judging by the dark shadows under her eyes.

Marianne nodded, holding out a hand along with a sympathetic smile. 'My name is Detective Inspector Marianne McGuire, from the British Transport Police. And this is my colleague, Detective Chief Inspector Paul Cullen.'

'Jenny Gossage. Michael's wife. We spoke on the phone,' Jenny said to Cullen.

Cullen nodded. 'Thank you for taking the time to speak with us.'

'Of course,' she said, absent-mindedly. 'Please, do come in.'

They followed her down a narrow hallway into a lovely lounge, where they took up seats on the cream sofa.

'My...our son, Oscar,' she said, picking up one of his toy cars from the floor, 'he's with his grandparents - my mum and dad - they live just down the road.'

'How old is Oscar?' Marianne asked.

'Three,' she answered. 'You would think he might be too young to understand what's happening, but he's not.' She looked at them both as she passed Oscar's toy from hand to hand. 'He knows that daddy isn't coming back.' Her brow furrowed deeply.

'I'm so sorry,' Cullen said, noticing that Marianne was gazing at a family photograph of the three of them, standing next to the famous sign at Land's End.

Jenny swallowed. 'Me too.'

'I'm afraid we need to ask some questions,' Cullen continued. 'Are you okay if we do this now? We won't be any longer than we need to.'

She nodded. 'Go ahead. You've got a job to do. I understand that. And you want to help, I'm sure.'

'We do want to help,' Cullen said. 'We want to bring Michael's killer to justice.'

Jenny shook her head. 'Killer...I just can't believe it, that anyone would want to kill Michael.'

She looked at Cullen and Marianne.

'Why would someone do this to him?'

'That's what we intend to find out,' Cullen replied.

'Just to warn you,' Marianne said gently, 'that some of the questions we ask might feel uncomfortable, or difficult to answer. But if you can tell us anything that might help, please don't hold back.'

'I can't think of anything that would explain this,' Jenny said, as Cullen watched her closely for any tells. It was difficult to read people at this stage of grief, most certainly, but he did wonder whether there was something there.

Something not quite right.

'That's okay,' Marianne continued. 'I'm sure that's more than likely the case. But sometimes even the most inconsequential thing might lead to something bigger, something that helps us to understand.'

Jenny nodded.

'Sometimes,' Marianne continued, 'even the people we are closest to can be living lives, doing things, have another side to them, that we don't fully know about or understand. And occasionally, these things can lead to horrible consequences. But we often find that the partner, family, can help to unlock the truth, even if it's just through voicing their suspicions that something hasn't been quite right.'

And there it was. A micro-expression of discomfort - her tongue protruding ever so slightly from her mouth, then in an instant, back.

'It can give us something to go after,' Marianne added.

But Jenny wasn't taking the bait yet.

Cullen would let Marianne ask the initial questions, giving him time to observe. Then if needed, he could move in, and their roles would switch.

'So, Michael worked in a local school,' Marianne began, deciding to take the workplace path first. It was less personal than going straight in for any family issues, warming up the interviewee for the potentially more uncomfortable questions to come.

Jenny nodded. 'Lady Margaret's Academy,' she replied, already looking a little more settled with the questioning. 'History teacher. And Head of Year 9. He's been...was there...for the last ten years. He loved his job.'

'So there's not been any problems with his work?' Marianne asked. 'No conflict with colleagues?'

She shook her head. 'Nothing.'

Cullen thought she was lying about that, but held back.

'If there were any issues, then it would be really helpful to know about them,' Marianne pressed gently, seemingly picking up on the same vibes as Cullen.

Jenny's tongue made another brief appearance as the two officers waited.

'Please, if there is anything...' Marianne tried again.

It was clear to both Marianne and Cullen that Jenny, brow now furrowed, was trying to decide whether to tell them something.

She put a hand to her head.

'At the weekend, Saturday afternoon,' she said finally, straightening in the chair. 'One of his colleagues, Chris Barrington, he's a friend of ours. He came around to the house while Michael was out at the leisure centre, swimming, and told me that Michael was...he was getting too close with one of the Year 12s. A girl called Poppy Jones. I don't mean he was doing anything wrong. He was just spending too much time with her, helping her with her studies. But people - staff and students - were starting to talk. He asked me to speak to Michael because he was worried it might get out of hand.'

'And did you speak to him?'

'Yes,' she said. 'I didn't go well. We ended up arguing. He told me it was none of my business, and if I didn't trust him, then that was my problem. That was yesterday evening, just before he disappeared. I went upstairs to bed early, we still weren't talking. When I woke up in the middle of the night, he wasn't in bed. But I thought he was just still angry, and might be downstairs sleeping on the sofa. I didn't think for a second that something awful had happened. But in the morning when he wasn't in the house, and he'd left his wallet, keys, phone, I called the police. Oh, God...'

She broke into sobs and Marianne reached across to place an arm around her shaking shoulders.

Jenny recovered her composure quickly and Marianne pulled back.

'I mean, we've been having a few problems over the past year,' Jenny said, dabbing her eyes and blowing her nose. 'We're not as close as we used to be. But isn't that what happens when you have children?'

Cullen thought of his own marriage, and how their daughter Amy had tested his relationship with Sarah to the limit. Children could certainly make a difference, sometimes positive, sometimes negative.

'So you didn't speak to your husband at all after you came up to bed that evening?' Cullen sought to confirm.

'No, I didn't.'

Cullen continued the questioning. 'And what time was that?'

'Just after nine. I came up to read and, you know, put a bit of space between us. I read for a bit. I could hear him downstairs, banging around. I think he was still angry. Then I must have fallen asleep and only woke up in the middle of the night, when he wasn't in bed.'

'So you don't know what time he left the house?' Cullen asked.

'No.'

Ending that way would take some time to get over, Cullen mused. This lady would be in for a tough time. Achieving justice would help though, and that is what they all had to focus on. 'Is there anything else you think might be relevant to what happened to Michael?'

There was something more, Cullen was sure of it.

'Anything at all?' Cullen tried again.

Jenny waited a few beats. 'A few months ago,' she began, 'I found out that...oh this is so difficult...I...'

'It's okay,' Cullen said, 'take your time.'

She nodded, taking a breath. 'I found out that, you know,

Michael had been viewing pornography, on his phone and computer. He was always on his phone, going into other rooms, slipping it into his pocket when I came in. I thought, because things hadn't been good for us, you know, romantically, that he might be seeing someone else, or going on dating sites, I don't know...'

Marianne, after some time as observer, re-joined the conversation. 'But it was watching videos?'

'Yes,' she said, exhaling. 'Well, more than that. He...'

She was still struggling, so they gave her the time she needed.

'He had used one site, subscribed...so he could...interact with the girl...ask her to do things...you know?'

Marianne and Cullen nodded.

'I knew these things existed,' Jenny continued, 'but I never thought my own husband would...maybe I was just being naive. He said it didn't mean anything, that it was just entertainment.'

'So you challenged him about it?' Marianne asked.

'Oh yes. Like I said, he laughed it off really, said it was just a bit of fun, but that if it upset me, he'd stop doing it. I said it did upset me, a lot. He said sorry and promised not to use the sites anymore.'

'And that's the way it was left?'

She held up her hands. 'We didn't talk about it again. But I kept on an eye on him in the house, and he seemed to be on his phone less. And things improved a bit romantically. So I hoped that maybe me asking about it had been enough to do the trick. I trusted him.'

Cullen sensed she wanted to say more.

'You really think that Michael could have known the person who killed him?' Jenny asked suddenly.

'It's something we have to consider very seriously,' Marianne replied.

'In many murder cases the victim knows the perpetrator,' Cullen said.

That hit home.

'The thing you said just before, about sometimes people having another side to them,' Jenny added. 'I would never have thought Michael would have used a site like that. And I wonder now about the girl at school - was it innocent? I'm wondering if there were other things that I didn't know about him - things that might explain what happened? What if he was doing other things?'

She looked at the two officers for help.

'That's what we'll do our very best to find out,' Cullen said. He could see how troubled she was. 'I know it's upsetting, thinking that the one you love could have been hiding something from you, potentially something serious.'

Jenny nodded sadly. 'I still don't see how any of this could lead to what happened. Does it make sense to you?'

'Not yet,' was Cullen's honest answer. 'But we'll work relentlessly until we find your husband's killer. It would be helpful if we could take a look at Michael's phone and computer, just in case there's anything that helps. I can arrange for one of my team to come and pick it up.'

'Sure, of course,' Jenny replied. 'I just hope I've been able to help.' Jenny looked at the two officers, asking the unspoken question as to whether what she had said was enough to satisfy them.

'You have,' Cullen said, simply, as he made to stand.

'We'll be in touch,' Marianne added, joining Cullen at his side.

'Thank you,' she smiled sadly. 'Thank you.'

# 11

*Monday afternoon*

SHAZNEY LOVED WORKING AT *HARMONY*, the beauty salon on the high street. She'd been there for two years now, since leaving college, and had loved every minute of it.

But the last week had been very different.

'Lovely to see you again, Mrs Hobart,' she smiled to the lady who had just had her nails done. 'Can we book you in for another appointment? Maybe in a couple of weeks?'

Always try and book the customer in for the next appointment, Harmony had impressed upon her when she had first started. That was the single most effective way to keep people's custom, and build the business.

'Yes, that would be lovely,' Mrs Hobart said, referring to her phone. 'How about the 16th?'

Shazney checked the booking sheet. 'We can do the same time as today.'

'Fantastic.'

'Great, I've got you booked in.'

Let them walk out of the door without that commitment, and there was always the risk that it might be for the last time.

Shazney mustered another smile. 'Have a lovely day.'

Once Mrs Hobart had left, with the salon mercifully devoid of both customers and other staff, Shazney dropped her pretence of positivity. Shoulders sagging, and biting back guilt and grief she retreated into the back room and put on the kettle.

Maybe a cup of strong instant coffee would help.

As the kettle boiled, she took the time to read through the email again from Adrian Spencer, the journalist who had been so persistent this past week or so.

She still didn't know how he had tracked her down, just days after Tyrone's death.

Her name had been in the news, and being a journalist he hadn't found it that difficult to get her email address.

She studied the words again on her phone.

He said that he wanted to help her to get justice and ensure that the police were held accountable for what had happened.

He would run a story about the case, to put pressure on the authorities.

'Why did I say yes?'

She swiped through to her reply, which she had hammered out at the height of her anger and despair.

'I want justice against Tyrone's murderer,' she had decreed.

Now Adrian Spencer had said that he'd got the detective to agree to meet with them both to discuss what had happened.

'I'm such a fool.'

This surely could only lead to her lies being revealed - how in the aftermath of Tyrone's death she had told that single, yet crucial untruth - both to the police and to her family and friends.

'I didn't say anything,' she had lied. 'I didn't tell the officer nothing.'

Except that she had. And she was now going to have to meet the one other person who knew this. She was going to have to look him in the eye when he knew that she had tried to pin the blame on him.

That was probably why he had agreed to the meeting with her and the journalist - to get that opportunity to face his accuser and extract the truth.

'I can't do this.'

Her fingers hovered over the reply button as she ran through the decision to end this here and now. But just as she did, a message from Adrian Spencer came through.

'How spooky,' she said to herself, clicking through to it.

'The police have unfortunately gone back on their word,' began the short message. 'They don't want to meet us. I'll be in touch again soon once I've decided what to do.'

She was surprised by just how good this made her feel. When the bell rang as someone entered the salon, she felt brighter.

Until she saw who it was.

~

'Harmony, lovely to see ya,' Carlton said, as he closed the door and twisted across the sign in the window to "closed".

He clicked the lock shut before straightening up his

towering six foot four inch frame. His baggy clothes hid a gym-sculpted body, and he pushed up a pair of RayBans to reveal his stone-hard eyes.

'You know you're not allowed here,' Shazney managed to say, her heart racing. As much as she hated to admit it, Carlton intimidated her to the core.

He was dangerous and unpredictable. She'd heard terrible stories from Tyrone about the things he had inflicted upon his enemies and competitors.

Yet until now he'd escaped the law.

'Yeah,' he said, 'but I don't see no Harmony here, do I?' He swaggered deeper into the salon, taking lingering looks at the equipment as if he was eying up something to buy.

'She'll be back soon,' Shazney lied. In fact, Harmony was at a dentist appointment and had entrusted Shazney with the salon until closing, given that Mrs Hobart was the last booking of the day.

'Well I'd better be quick then,' he smiled, revealed the gold capped front tooth that he had paid to be fitted as a fashion statement.

Shazney took a breath. 'What do you want?'

Carlton hopped gymnastically into one of the large salon chairs, sending it spinning like a fairground waltzer. 'What do you recommend?'

'You want a treatment?' she asked in disbelief.

'Yeah, girl. This is a beauty salon, ain't it? Then give me some beauty treatment.'

Shazney really wasn't sure what to do. How could she rid herself of him without escalating the situation? 'Harmony won't like this. I think it's better if you go.'

Carlton smiled, remaining steadfast in the chair. 'You know, Shazney, I really enjoyed the party yesterday.'

'Party?'

'Yeah, man, Tyrone's big bash. Pity he couldn't have been there to enjoy it himself.'

Shazney wanted to hit out at him. 'Just leave.'

'I've got to say, girl, I was a bit hurt that you didn't come over to say hello,' he continued. 'I mean, me and the boys, we made the effort, to pay our respects...'

'You didn't show any respect,' she said without hesitation.

Carlton looked puzzled. 'What? Because me and da boys were havin' a good time, a good laugh, init? Don't think I didn't see you and Harmony giving us the evils.' He spun three hundred and sixty degrees in the chair, legs outstretched. 'What did you want me to do, girl, cry like a baby?' He came to a stop, his eyes daring Shazney to respond.

'You're poison,' she said. 'Please, leave, now. You've done enough damage.'

He shook his head. 'You see, I get the feelin' that you're blamin' me for what happened to your boyfriend. But it wasn't me who chased him under that bus, was it?'

She bit her tongue.

'It was the pig,' he continued. 'He chased him down and killed poor Tyrone just because of the colour of his skin. Ain't that so?'

She continued to keep her counsel. Maybe if she didn't rise to the bait, he would get bored and leave. But unfortunately, he wasn't finished with her yet.

'Don't you feel angry, Shazney?' he asked. 'That Tyrone was murdered?'

'He wasn't murdered.'

'That's not what you said a few days ago,' he said, correctly.

'It was an accident.'

'That's not what your daddy thinks.' He smiled.

'Leave my father out of this.'

He held up his hands. 'Hey, girl, he came to me.' He gauged her reaction. 'Wanna know why?'

'Please leave.' She moved over to the front door, clicked across the lock and opened it, pushing down her anxiety to try and act decisively in the face of this bully boy. 'I'm busy.'

Carlton rose slowly from the chair. 'Your daddy has asked me to right a wrong,' he said, moving right up close to her so that their faces were only inches apart.

*My God. Is that why her father had been talking to them?*

'Tyrone was a soldier,' Carlton continued. 'One of my own.' He thumped his chest. 'He was slain in battle. It don't matter whether he was fleein' like a coward, like some kid runnin' across the main road without his mummy to help him dodge the traffic.' He thumped his chest hard again. 'He was one of mine, girl, and I'm going to avenge his death.'

'Stay out of it,' she said, even as she was cowering from his angry spittle.

'Stay out of it?' he laughed. 'I'm already in it, girl, and I'm lovin' it, just lovin' it!' He pointed his fingers into a gun shape as he left the salon and directed it at Shazney's head with three rapid movements as he closed an eye across an imaginary sight. 'Boom! Boom! Boom!'

# 12

*Monday afternoon*

'What do you think?' Cullen asked, as he and DI McGuire said goodbye to Jenny Gossage and made their way back along the road to the train station.

The sun was out and the light dappled through the trees that lined the street. 'Anything significant from our conversation with Jenny?' Cullen added.

'I'm not sure,' Marianne replied, crossing the road as a taxi let them past. 'I mean, her husband watched porn and didn't tell her about it. Isn't that what a lot of men do? I know my brothers and their mates were always looking at stuff like that. Doesn't seem that out of the ordinary to me.'

Cullen agreed. 'The thing with the woman, though. The subscribing thing, where he was asking her to do things. That doesn't seem as normal?'

Marianne actually laughed. 'I think you're a little behind

the times, Paul,' she said. 'I'm afraid that kind of thing is pretty normal these days.'

He turned to her without slowing his stride. 'Really?'

'Oh yes. Have you not heard of My Fans? It's an app where you can subscribe to watch people doing anything – and I mean, anything.'

He shook his head. He wasn't really a follower of the latest crazes with regards to apps, and didn't use his smart phone for much more than making calls, checking travel times and keeping up with the rugby results. The rest of that stuff just seemed like at best a massive waste of time, and at worst a gateway to trouble.

Anyway, he couldn't afford to spend half his day head down in a screen, even if he'd wanted to.

'It's probably the app Michael was using,' Marianne said. 'You pay a certain amount each month to a creator, and for that you get access to their content.'

'Their content?'

'It's not always dodgy,' Marianne explained, correctly interpreting Cullen's reaction. 'My cousin, back in Ireland, she does gigs from her bedroom on the acoustic guitar. She's got quite a following, several hundred people, who pay per month to watch her perform.'

'Impressive.'

'But a lot of the stuff on there is towards the more dodgy end,' she admitted. 'People can earn thousands of pounds through subscriptions, taking off their clothes, performing sexual actions, having...'

'I get the idea,' he interrupted.

'It's really big among university students,' Marianne continued, 'to clear their debts and make a not insignificant amount of money on top.'

Cullen's thoughts turned immediately to his daughter, Amy, at university in Bristol. Surely she would never do such a thing? He shook the thought away.

'Sounds dangerous - like you might attract the wrong sort of attention.'

'It can happen. There was a case in Scotland a few months ago, where a client tracked down one of the creators and assaulted her.'

They continued their walk as Cullen thought some more about Michael and his behaviour.

*Could it be related to his death?*

He thought back to the message stuffed into his trousers.

*Soon everyone will know what you really are!*

'Penny for your thoughts,' Marianne said.

'Oh, I'm just wondering if there is any connection with his behaviour. Do you think Jenny was holding anything back?'

'I don't think so.'

'Me neither. So I'm pinning my hopes on the phone or computer. Or the school. Either Chris Barrington, the teacher who spoke to Jenny, or the sixth form student - if they'll let us speak with her.'

Despite being only a fifteen minute walk away from their present location, it was too late in the afternoon to visit the school where Michael had taught. They had however called through to arrange an appointment with Chris Barrington for the next day. Although he had offered to talk to them this evening, they wanted to speak to him on site, when the pupils were present, as it would also be good to chat to the student, as informally as possible.

They hadn't asked in advance about speaking to Poppy Jones - they would broach that when they got there, and see how things went.

'We'll have to tread carefully,' Marianne noted. 'With Poppy.'

'Yes, definitely.'

~

CULLEN USED the remains of the day to catch up on work back at Headquarters and arrange collection of Michael Gossage's phone and computer. He also checked in with DI Lomax to update him on developments before grabbing an evening meal at a lovely little Italian restaurant just off Euston Road.

He didn't mind eating alone, as it gave him time to think.

About everything.

On the ten minute walk back to the hotel, he called Tony's wife, Brenda, to see how things were. She was sounding a lot brighter, and looking forward to her husband returning home in the coming days. Cullen didn't mention the retirement word, but wondered whether Tony's decision to hang up his badge was the real reason for her happy mood.

He'd just reached the Excelsior Hotel, his residence of choice for the past few weeks when his phone rang. The number wasn't linking to any of his contacts.

'Detective Cullen.'

At first the voice didn't register, but then he realised.

'Sir Kenneth?'

'Indeed. I saw the report in today's news,' he said. 'The case of the man on the tracks.'

Sir Kenneth New, the billionaire businessman and entrepreneur was currently at the centre of a significant police investigation into multiple allegations of sexual misconduct going back decades. His accusers, including Natalie Long, the friend of Cullen's daughter Amy, had come forward to reveal a vile pattern of behaviour from the man once lauded for his business successes and philanthropy.

*Why was he calling?*

'Yes.' Cullen knew that it was being reported in the media – he and Danny had reviewed some of the material back at the office, as it was always useful to keep abreast of what the press were saying. The London Daily Post had it on page two of their early evening edition, the online clickbait news site London Lines was full of lurid speculation, and social media was alight with rumours that ranged from a serial killer to suicide.

Michael Gossage's name was well and truly out there.

'How can I help?' Cullen asked.

'I would like to speak with you, urgently. About the case. Meet me at New House, first thing tomorrow morning. It will be worth your while, Detective Cullen, I promise you.'

# 13

*Monday evening*

CARLTON'S WORDS had been playing on Shazney's mind for the rest of the evening.

What the hell had her dad said to him?

She still lived at the family home, only able to dream at the moment about moving out and gaining full independence - she was a prisoner of the London housing market, which locked out anyone who didn't have significant amounts of cash.

She lay on her bed, plugged into her smart phone as the music played loudly, with Beyonce pounding at her insides. She flipped over onto her front, legs dangled off the bed, and crashed her head into her pillow.

Her mum was downstairs, preparing the evening meal, awaiting the arrival of her father from his shift. He'd worked on the London buses for thirty-five years, ever since coming to the UK from Jamaica. A proud man, he'd always cared and looked out for his family, but this time Shazney wondered whether he'd gone too far.

Shazney looked at the time. It was half past six. He would be arriving home any minute. She slipped off her headphones and waited at the top of the landing.

The door unlocked just a few seconds later.

He was always bang on time.

'Daddy,' she called, from the top of the stairs. 'Daddy.'

Malcolm Powell appeared at the bottom, and gave her a warm but tired smile. The long days driving around London were taking their toll on him. 'Are you okay? Things go well at the salon today?'

'Yes, Daddy,' she said.

'Why don't you come down, be with me and your mother? It will do you good, to be around other people. I'm worried you're spending too much time on your own at the moment.'

'Can you come up for a second?' she asked. 'I've got something to ask you.'

He climbed the stairs, followed her into the bedroom and sat down next to her on the end of the bed, knees touching, just like they had done for all those years, reading bedtime stories.

He patted her leg. 'Ask away, Angel.'

Shazney swallowed. 'Harmony left me in charge of the salon this afternoon.'

'Wow,' he smiled, 'that's wonderful. Didn't I tell you, you've made a very positive impression with Harmony. She'll be making you a partner soon.'

Shazney laughed in embarrassment. 'I don't think so.'

'No, you'll be setting up your own salon in the future, I can see it.' He gestured. 'Shazney's Super Salon,' I can picture it now.

Shazney smiled. 'It does sound good.'

'It will happen,' he stated confidently. 'Now, time to go downstairs to eat,' he said, starting to rise from the bed, 'and celebrate with your mother and her wonderful jerk chicken.'

'Carlton visited the salon,' she said, causing her father to immediately sit back down.

His face darkened. 'Oh. I thought that Harmony had banned him from...'

'She had...has. But,' she smiled uncomfortably, 'she wasn't there, and you know Carlton, he does what he likes.'

'He didn't do anything to you, did he?' he asked, horrified. 'Because if he did, I swear, I'll...'

'Daddy, he didn't do anything. Apart from being his usual self. But he said something that's got me worried.'

'You two, tea's on the table!' Shazney's mother shouted from downstairs.

'Down in a second,' Malcolm replied, his face full of worry. He turned to Shazney. 'What did he say to you?'

'He said he was going to get justice for Tyrone.' She watched her father, to see his reaction. He tried to play a poker face, but there was a flicker of recognition. 'He said you'd asked him.' Shazney's stomach turned at the confirmation that he knew what this comment had meant.

'Keep away from Carlton,' he said, softly but sternly. 'Keep away from him and his people.'

'But Daddy, what have you...'

He put up a finger. 'When you began to have relations with Tyrone, what did I say to you?'

Shazney remembered their conversation well. It was not a pleasant experience. 'You told me to keep away from him.'

'Yes, I did. And did you listen?'

'No.'

'And look at where it led, Angel.' His voice softened. 'I wanted to protect you, from those kind of people. I knew what would happen. That no good would come of it. But you didn't listen to me, and you're now suffering because of it. For that I am truly sorry. It breaks my heart to see you this way....' He stammered with his words, and Shazney realised to her shock that he was crying.

She'd only ever seen her father cry once before, at the news that his mother had died, back in Jamaica. Apart from that one incident, he had maintained the strong fatherly persona that he had so carefully cultivated.

'Daddy, it's okay,' she said, placing a hand on his wet cheek.

He recovered quickly, embarrassed. 'You could have been killed too,' he said. 'The chase out of the station, from the police officer, you could have been together. He would have taken you across that busy road, and you would have gone, wouldn't you?'

She shrugged, thinking that he was probably right. Caught up in the moment, hand in hand with Tyrone, she could picture herself fleeing out of the station concourse, down the path and blindly braving the traffic with the man she loved. 'I don't know...'

She'd been a fool.

She leant her head against his chest, and he placed a hand on her.

'He would have led you to your death,' he said. 'And I would never have forgiven myself.'

'It was my fault,' she said. 'It's all my fault.'

'No,' he said. 'I should have been firmer with you, made sure you did as I said.'

'But...'

'Are you coming down, the tea's getting cold!' came another shout from downstairs.

'Your mother thinks the same,' he continued. 'She blames me.'

'I don't think she...'

'She does,' he interrupted. 'She's made that very clear to me. I failed you.'

Shazney raised her head. 'Daddy, stop it, please.'

His face was hard.

'What did you speak to Carlton about? At the event on Sunday?'

'Nothing,' he said.

'You were talking to them about something,' she pressed.

'I was telling them to behave themselves,' he replied. 'Warning them not to be their usual selves and make things worse for you and Tyrone's family. The way they were laughing and joking, like they were at a party, it was disrespectful.'

Shazney wasn't sure she believed his explanation. Not after what Carlton had said in the salon. But then maybe it was Carlton who was playing games, making her doubt what was happening, twisting the knife.

*After all, who should she believe - a gangster, or her own father?*

And yet, the expression on her father's face still seeded doubt.

She tried again. 'At the funeral, you said that the man who did that to Tyrone and me would pay a very heavy price. What did you mean?'

'You were upset. I was upset. They were just words spoken in anger.'

'Really?'

'Really. Angel, I'm a humble bus driver, what do you think I'm going to do, really?'

'I was worried that...'

'That I was going to do something stupid?' He patted her leg. 'Angel, I've worked hard for nearly forty years, all those hours on the buses, travelling around this noisy and busy city. I've been out at dawn, back in the dark. I've battled through the wind and the rain, snow and ice. I've dealt with the best and worst of people, and everyone in between. I've been praised, thanked, shouted out, racially abused, threatened. And next year I finally, after all those years of toil, will be retiring. Do you really think I want to throw that all away and spend my remaining days in jail?' He raised an eyebrow.

'No,' she admitted.

'I have plans,' he said, looking towards the door just in case Shazney's mother had given up shouting and decided to drag them down for their food. 'Secret plans, that your mother doesn't know about. Your mother and I, we're going to Jamaica next year. As soon as I retire, we're off for three weeks, to see the homeland.' He was beaming. They hadn't been back for many years now and hadn't seen their extended family for too long. 'And we're gong to stay in luxury,' he continued. 'One of the top hotels. I've got some brochures.'

'That sounds amazing.'

'You see,' he smiled. 'I 'ain't planning on getting in any trouble, Angel. I want my holiday of a lifetime.'

'That's good,' she said, now persuaded that she had been led down the wrong path by Carlton's lies. 'I just want to move on now from everything.'

'That's so good to hear, Angel,' he said. 'Now we'd better

get ourselves downstairs, before your mother comes to get us.'

Everything felt fine for that moment. But then the ever-present feeling of guilt re-emerged. Could she really move on from everything if she didn't admit to her lie about what she had had said to the police officer? 'Daddy...'

'Yes, Angel?'

Something stopped her from continuing with her confession. Maybe now that things seemed sorted, she could really put the dreadful events behind her and move on with her life. The guilt would fade, surely, and time would heal.

'I love you,' she said simply.

# PART II

# 14

*Tuesday morning*

CULLEN STEPPED over the threshold of New House, an uber-posh Edwardian building in London's exclusive Mayfair district. Owned by Sir Kenneth New, the house was an entertaining and hotel space for his company, Brand New, as well as being one of his several private residences. Cullen took in the ornate surroundings of the reception area, which was like the poshest hotel you could imagine. The marble floor was so polished it reflected like a mirror and a grandfather clock kept time over in the corner.

The last time he was here, just a couple of weeks ago, it was to investigate the disappearance of Natalie Long. Now he'd been drawn back to this house because of another case.

He reported to reception and took a closer look at the grandfather clock while he waited.

'Detective Cullen, so glad you could make it!' Sir Kenneth

said, approaching from behind with a smile and proffered hand.

Cullen smiled tightly as they shook hands.

'Let's go through into my study,' Sir Kenneth said, gesturing for Cullen to follow. 'Would you like a drink, Detective?' he asked, over his shoulder. 'I can do any beverage, alcoholic or non.'

'I'm fine,' Cullen replied.

Sir Kenneth waved his reply away. 'Please, I'd like you to taste the new wine that's just come in. It's from one of my vineyards, a lovely little place in Gloucestershire. Award winning.'

'I don't drink on the job,' Cullen replied, mildly irked by Sir Kenneth's dismissal of his wishes. Sir Kenneth was the kind of person who always got his own way, by one means or another. He'd seen it before. Most often it was men against women, and he didn't like it one bit.

'Oh come on, Detective, please.' Sir Kenneth diverted suddenly into a side room, which was stocked with more alcohol than your average pub. He moved across to a bottle of wine and expertly poured a glass, handing it to Cullen. 'Go on,' he prompted, 'please. I would be offended if you didn't at least have a sip.'

He looked on expectantly.

'Well I wouldn't want to offend you,' Cullen said, with a hint of sarcasm. He touched the liquid to his lips, allowing the taste to hit.

He really didn't like wine.

Give him a pint of mild any day, standing on the terraces watching a hard game of rugby.

'Well?' Sir Kenneth asked. 'What do you think, Detective? Good.'

'Nice.'

Sir Kenneth actually looked crestfallen. So much so that Cullen had to stifle a mischievous smile.

'Nice?'

'Yes, nice. Very nice. Now,' he said, handing the still almost-full glass back to his deflated host, 'what was it you wanted to talk to me about? You said it would be worth my while.'

'Indeed,' Sir Kenneth said, still recovering from the wine incident. He placed the glass down on a nearby table. 'I do want to speak to you about something extremely important.'

'Go on.'

'It's about your dead body. The man on the tracks. I think I might be able to help. I think I might know why he was killed.'

Now he had Cullen's full attention.

~

'PLEASE, take a seat, Detective, and I'll tell you all.'

As much as Cullen didn't like being beholden to this man, he was intrigued about the unexpected development. 'I'm all ears,' he said, taking a seat opposite his host.

He watched Sir Kenneth as the billionaire waited several beats, stroking his beard, seemingly enjoying the fact he had Cullen hooked.

'Detective Cullen,' he said, at last. 'Before we discuss the issue at hand, I'd like to talk about another matter of great importance to me.'

Cullen gave a subtle shake of the head, revealing his thoughts. He'd suspected that this would come up, and was already fully prepared to shut down that particular line of conversation.

Sir Kenneth checked himself, evidently noticing Cullen's reaction. But then he continued after Cullen gave him some rope.

'All of these accusations,' Sir Kenneth said, leaning forward with his hands now clasped in front of him. 'There is no truth in them, Detective.'

Cullen already knew that Sir Kenneth was denying any wrong doing.

'You need to tell this to the investigation team, not me,' Cullen replied.

Sir Kenneth sat back and actually smiled a little. 'Detective, I have told them, many, many times, believe me.'

*I don't believe you*, Cullen wanted so much to shoot back.

'Well you will probably have your day in court,' Cullen said. 'The wheels of justice will turn and the truth will out.'

Sir Kenneth laughed bitterly. 'You really think so? I know friends who have gone to jail for crimes that they did not commit. Good friends who have been hounded and vilified by accusers whose lies have been believed and acted upon.'

'Sir Kenneth...'

'There is an agenda,' Sir Kenneth continued, cutting across Cullen. 'There is an agenda, globally, to take down people like me.' He was angry and perturbed. 'People are jealous, they look at the success of others, and they compare it with their own lives, and instead of using this as a motivation to better themselves, they seek to bring those with success down to their knees.'

It was interesting seeing Sir Kenneth talk about this. He seemed to really believe what he was saying. Either he really didn't think he had done anything wrong, even though he had, or he was actually the victim here.

But there was no way Cullen thought that this guy was a victim. Not that he was going to engage in this.

'I'm afraid I can't comment on the case,' Cullen said.

Although the investigation was being led by the Met rather than Cullen's British Transport Police, it would be extremely unprofessional and potentially damaging to the case to say anything that could be used by Sir Kenneth or his lawyers to suggest any bias in the process.

'I'm sure you understand,' Cullen added.

Sir Kenneth nodded. 'Okay,' he said, 'but I just wanted you to know, that I'm not guilty of anything. Your daughter's friend Natalie, for example, she was mistaken, she misinterpreted my intentions. She jumped to conclusions, which frankly, were wrong, very wrong.'

'Sir Kenneth...' Cullen tried.

'Do you know the details of what happened with Natalie?'

'We can't discuss this now,' he said, although in truth he had heard the full details of what had happened that day in Sir Kenneth's apartment, within this very building. Cullen's daughter Amy had relayed what Natalie had told her.

'It was innocent,' Sir Kenneth said, again annoying Cullen with his insistence at making his case. 'I have a bad shoulder, from a riding accident several years ago. It suddenly began to hurt, and I asked Natalie for help to ease the pain - to press into the muscle and release the pain. I can't do it myself. I need someone to help...'

'You need to tell this to someone else.'

'I asked Natalie to press on my shoulder, and when the pain referred down to my back, which it invariably does, then I asked her to help with that too. I'm afraid she confused my request for medical help with some sort of...sexual intent.' Sir Kenneth's face twisted in disgust at the idea.

*You were lying there on the bed in just your underwear,* Cullen had wanted to shoot back.

'Like I said, I'm not involved in this case,' Cullen brushed off. 'If it had happened on the transport network, then yes, but it didn't.'

'And the other women,' Sir Kenneth continued, 'some are similarly confused about their situation, while others, I'm afraid, are just out to get me, for a number of reasons - none of which mean that I am a pervert.'

'As I told you, I can't...'

Sir Kenneth plowed on. 'And this isn't just about damage to my business. In fact, my businesses will get through this. It's my charity work, Detective, it's already having a tremendously negative impact on the good work that my charities are trying to do. Many, many people around the world will suffer as a result of this. People don't want to work with someone accused of such things. I mean, I am known globally for my work on women's rights!' Anger flared in his eyes. 'I am a philanthropist!'

It was really time to end this.

'I'm going to have to shut down this line of conversation now,' Cullen stated, more firmly. 'It isn't appropriate.'

Sir Kenneth wasn't prepared to give up just yet. 'Aren't you interested in what I have to say about your man on the tracks?'

'I am,' Cullen replied, fully aware that Sir Kenneth may well think he could use his information as some kind of bargaining chip. 'If you want to tell me.'

'And if I help you, then you can help...'

'I'd better go now,' Cullen said, getting to his feet and

sliding a hand into his jacket pocket. 'Please, if you want to speak to me, you can get me on this number.'

He handed the contact card to a surprised Sir Kenneth, who gazed up at the officer. 'But don't you want to hear what I have to say?'

'I do. But not with strings,' Cullen stated, matter-of-factly, as he moved towards the door. 'I can show myself out,' he said. 'I know the way.'

'But Detective...'

Cullen strode purposefully towards the exit, nodding a professional goodbye to the girl on reception.

'Detective Cullen!' Sir Kenneth shouted, as he hurried after him. 'Please, don't leave yet.'

Cullen turned with an inner smile. 'Yes?'

Sir Kenneth was breathless, from exertion or panic Cullen wasn't sure.

'I really need to tell you what I know.'

'Without strings?'

'No strings,' he said, catching his breath. He glanced over at the receptionist, who retreated into the back office. 'I just want to help.'

Cullen doubted that very much, but still...

'Let's get down to business then,' Cullen said, much to Sir Kenneth's obvious relief.

# 15

*Tuesday morning*

CULLEN AND SIR KENNETH returned to the study and settled back into their seats. Cullen refused another offer of a drink.

'So how do you think you can help?' Cullen started, hoping that Sir Kenneth had now got the message that any more talk of the sexual assault allegations would now be well and truly off limits.

'I have already been helping,' Sir Kenneth replied cryptically.

Irked, Cullen bit down on his annoyance. He really didn't want to spend any more time than necessary in this guy's company. He was a complete creep with a superiority complex, who thought he was smooth but was just not. 'Sorry, I don't understand...'

'Your Operation Archangel,' Sir Kenneth replied. 'A very worthy endeavour, very worthy indeed. The safety of girls and women in London, particularly on the underground, is quite a passion of mine.'

'Is it?'

'Oh yes, Detective. Safety on the transport network, for women and girls in particular, is something I am very passionate about. Do you know why?'

'I'm all ears.'

Cullen couldn't quite believe the man accused of multiple sexual offences was taking this line. He certainly had a way about him. Did he really believe what he was saying?

'My young niece was assaulted on an underground train last year,' Sir Kenneth said. 'She was in a carriage, late at night, travelling back from a party. Three men cornered her and tried to pressure her into going back to their flat. They were very insistent, but my niece is strong-willed like her uncle. Unfortunately when she resisted, they assaulted her.'

'I'm really sorry to hear that,' Cullen said.

Sir Kenneth nodded. 'The carriage was quiet, there was no-one there to help, no-one she could turn to. Those men, they knew that, and they took full advantage.'

'Were they...'

'Caught?' Sir Kenneth said, finishing Cullen's sentence. 'I'm afraid not.'

'I'm sorry to hear that.' Cullen, unfortunately, wasn't surprised. One would think with all the cameras on the network, identifying perpetrators would be easy, but it often wasn't. As his friend Anthony Braddock had explained on more than one occasion, this was for a variety of reasons.

'They never identified those three men.'

Sometimes it was to do with the positioning of the cameras, sometimes it was the quality of the image, and sometimes it was because the offenders knew how to evade detection, whether that be by shielding themselves amongst the crowds, hiding their face using scarfs and hoods, or choosing their place of offence carefully to ensure the cameras wouldn't capture their crime.

'So they were able to get away with what they'd done.' Sir Kenneth said. 'The knowledge that they were still out there, free to roam, it really affected my niece. Do you know, she's not been on the tube since. She tried, but she couldn't.'

'I'm really sorry,' Cullen repeated. 'We know that too many people get away with it, and we need to do better. And that's what Operation Archangel is about.'

'I'm sure you're trying your best, Detective,' Sir Kenneth replied, 'but I'm afraid it's just not enough. Stepping up patrols, increasing visibility of the police, more plain clothes officers, I mean, it's great, but it just scratches at the surface of the problem. It can never be effective. There aren't enough officers in your force to make enough of a difference.'

Cullen wanted to beg to differ, but there was truth to what he was saying. 'We're making a positive difference,' was all he could manage in response.

'A positive difference, but a significant difference?'

Cullen mused on that question, but before he could answer, a newly emboldened Sir Kenneth filled the gap.

'I realised,' he said, 'that to really make a difference, it isn't enough to rely on the police - as I said, it's a simple numbers game. Instead, you need to harness the greatest resource that London has - its people.'

Cullen let him continue.

'And that's what MayDay is all about.'

'You created MayDay?' Cullen said. It was only in the past few weeks that the app had been brought to his attention. Its popularity had sky-rocketed with commuters on the tube, who valued the sense of security it gave them.

Users who felt in danger could press a help button that would send out a signal to fellow users in the nearby vicinity. The app could direct those users to the location of the person who had called for help, who were then able to come to their aid.

On the face of it, people thought it was a great idea.

But as he had voiced to Maggie Ferguson, the concept of calling on fellow citizens to intervene in potentially dangerous incidents worried Cullen, who feared the unintended consequences of promoting a vigilante culture.

And although there hadn't been an incidences yet of problems caused by the app, it was early days.

Cullen felt it was just a matter of time before something bad happened.

'I've funded its development and promotion,' Sir Kenneth said proudly. 'It was developed by someone who I think you may have met, Detective – Krishna Chatterjee.'

'Krishna Chatterjee?'

'Yes.'

Cullen did indeed know the name. Krishna had, along with Natalie Long, been one of the people who had been invited by Sir Kenneth and his company to take part in an Apprentice-style competition - with the prize to work with Sir Kenneth. Following Natalie's disappearance, Cullen had interviewed Krishna as a suspect, although he had ultimately been uninvolved in the incident.

'You knew Krishna before he took part in the competition here?'

'I started working with Krishna some months before,' Sir Kenneth confirmed. 'I was impressed by the dating app he had developed, Vicinity, and approached him about putting together my concept for MayDay.'

'But if Krishna already worked for you, then why was he taking part in the event here?'

'Because he wanted to show he could win it,' Sir Kenneth said, 'and move into the foreground, away from the developmental side of things. But the problem was...is...that Krishna isn't cut out for a front-of-stage role like that. He is a brilliant mind, when it comes to imagination and technological skills. He's also supremely confident, but slightly deluded, about his own abilities beyond that. I'm afraid when it comes to personal skills and charisma, he falls down badly. But he was insistent that he could do it, so I gave him the opportunity to fail.'

'That's very kind of you,' Cullen quipped.

Sir Kenneth smiled as he opened up his palms. 'It was for the best, Detective. Krishna now realises that he needs to focus on his strengths, and that's what he is doing. He's done a fantastic job with MayDay.'

'So what does my current case have to do with your app?' Cullen asked, keen to get to the nub of the situation.

'Well,' Sir Kenneth smiled. 'I read about the incident on the tracks, and decided I might be able to help. Do you know that as well as its alert system, MayDay is also an intelligence gathering mechanism?'

Cullen shook his head.

'We've been beta testing it for a few weeks now,' Sir Kenneth explained. 'Users can take photos or videos of individuals and those files are uploaded to our secure cloud server. They can then be used as evidence for action.'

Cullen wasn't convinced about the legality of that, from a

data gathering and storage perspective, but he was interested, so didn't interupt.

'But more importantly,' Sir Kenneth continued, 'the database can then be combined with our artificial intelligence technology to spot patterns of behaviour by individuals and alert our team. Taken in isolation these could be quite low level incidents. The kind of thing that might be missed, or even worse, dismissed. Standing that bit too close behind a lady, brushing up against them, for example. But we know, don't we Detective, that small crimes often precede bigger offences?'

'Sometimes.'

'Your man on the tracks. We ran his image through our database yesterday afternoon, just as a test...we didn't expect to find anything really. But as it was you leading the investigation, we thought, why not, let's give it a go, see if we can be of service.'

Sir Kenneth let things hang for a few seconds.

'And?' Cullen said at last.

Another few seconds of infuriating suspense as the two men eyed one another. 'And we came up with an interesting result.'

'He was on the database?'

'He was indeed. Your man on the tracks was an offender on the network.'

'He didn't have anything on his record,' Cullen revealed. 'No arrests. No cautions.'

'I'm not surprised,' Sir Kenneth replied. 'His behaviour was towards the lower end of the scale. The three reports that were linked to his image were from our third party users, who had seen him doing something that they felt was suspicious. Two of the incidents, from a couple of weeks ago, are where they saw him brush a hand and linger against a fellow passenger. The other incident, last week, is a potential upskirt event, using his camera.'

'So none of those incidents involved a report by the alleged victim?'

'No. They were likely unaware.'

That was definitely plausible. The tube was at times so crowded that people could get away with things like this.

'Are you sure it's the same man?'

'One hundred percent certain,' Sir Kenneth replied. 'Our AI doesn't get it wrong.'

Sir Kenneth watched on in fascination as Cullen processed what he had just been told.

'What are you thinking, Detective?'

'Can I have those files?'

'Of course,' Sir Kenneth nodded. 'As I said, we want to help.'

'Are they time-stamped?'

Sir Kenneth nodded.

'Good.' He would get Anthony Braddock on the case. With precise timings, he might be able to come up with more footage, even if it was just of the most recent incident.

Sir Kenneth sat forward. 'Do you think this man's behaviour could be connected to his murder, Detective?'

'I don't know,' was Cullen's honest answer.

But did he suspect it?

Most definitely.

# 16

*Tuesday morning*

'Back here again,' Cullen said as Detective Inspector Marianne McGuire met him in the reception area of the National CCTV Headquarters, just before lunch on Tuesday morning.

'We must stop meeting like this,' she replied.

Cullen took a seat opposite the television that was still playing the same "making of" video on an endless loop.

'They really need to get some new releases on here though,' Marianne joked, 'I mean, the choice of movies is just terrible.'

Cullen laughed as he looked around for Anthony Braddock, the head of the CCTV Operations Hub. In his usual style of bait and hook, the ever-teasing Braddock had trailed a potentially vital discovery from the footage that Sir Kenneth had provided to Cullen.

And Cullen was desperate to find out what it was.

'You think there might be a breakthrough?' Marianne said, having been briefed on the phone just an hour ago by Cullen about the morning's meeting with Sir Kenneth New.

'Braddock never undersells his findings,' Cullen replied.

'Exciting,' she smiled. But then Cullen noted a micro-expression, a frown.

'What's up?'

Marianne hesitated. 'It's personal,' she said, at last.

Cullen nodded and didn't press any more.

'I met up with Danny last night,' she revealed, her face looking like she was confessing to some awful crime.

'Oh, that's great,' Cullen replied, pleasantly surprised. 'It's great you're back in touch.'

'Yes,' she nodded, looking far from convinced.

Cullen watched as she played with the inside of her mouth with her tongue, contemplating something. 'What is it?'

'Did you set it up?' she asked, her face hardening slightly.

'Set what up?' he said, not knowing what on earth she was talking about.

'It's okay,' she said, softening again, but still thinking deeply about something.

Cullen didn't want to leave this hanging. 'Set what up, Marianne?'

She looked right at him. 'I went to visit Tony yesterday at the hospital, and just a few minutes after I arrived, Danny turned up. That's how we got talking, and you know, we decided to go out last night to discuss a few things.'

Cullen nodded. 'You think I set it up that you'd be there at the same time? Do I look like a matchmaker?'

The usually calm and collected Detective Inspector actually blushed, so much so that Cullen regretted his directness, even if it was joke.

'Sorry,' she said. 'It's just that later on, Danny and I, we both realised that Tony had asked us to come at the same time. Us meeting there, it wasn't a co-incidence.'

'Well, I never had Tony down as an old romantic,' Cullen smiled. 'Maybe his near death experience has changed the guy.' He shook his head. 'And you thought I was in on the act?'

Marianne shrugged. 'Well, yes, maybe.'

'And you resent colleagues sticking their noses into your personal life?'

'Something like that,' she smiled. 'Although I guess I'll have to forgive Tony, given his current condition.'

'And if it had been me? Would I have been forgiven?'

'Definitely not,' she joked.

'Fair enough. In that case, I won't ask how last night went.' Cullen looked around again for Anthony Braddock, feigning disinterest with Marianne's love life. In fact, his close friendship to both Marianne and Danny meant that he was interested, but not in a nosey way. These two people deserved to be happy together.

He cared.

'It went well,' she said. 'Really well.'

Cullen turned back to her, resisting a smile.

'I'm glad we met up,' Marianne continued. 'We said a lot of things that needed to be said, to clear the air. And it felt natural, being with him. Actually, it felt great - really great. We're meeting up again, tonight.'

'That's good,' Cullen said, feeling like a dad who dared not to show too much excitement at his daughter's choice of man, in case his blessing scuppered things.

'I have a good feeling about it,' she added.

'Sounds like you need to thank Uncle Tony,' Cullen said.

She smiled. 'Maybe I will.'

Just then, Anthony Braddock appeared, swiping through the security gates.

'Back again?' Braddock smiled, striding towards them.

Cullen and Marianne were already on their feet. Braddock pumped Cullen's hand excitedly, beaming in a way that set Cullen's expectations even higher. 'You must have good news,' Cullen said, trying to get something out of him.

'I do,' Braddock said, now shaking hands with Marianne. 'Nice to see you again so soon, Detective Inspector McGuire.'

'And you,' Marianne replied.

'Right,' Braddock said. 'Let's get down to business, officers.'

And with that they followed him through the gates and up towards the CCTV Hub.

'PLEASE, TAKE A SEAT,' Braddock gestured. 'You may not have met my new colleague, Mike?'

'A pleasure,' Cullen said, nodding a hello at Anthony Braddock's technician.

'Mike's been going through the footage with a fine tooth comb. It's been a labour of love for the past day.'

Mike smiled. 'It took a bit of looking at, but the results are worth it.'

'They really are,' Braddock confirmed.

Cullen glanced across to Marianne, while crossing his fingers that this would be as good as trailed. 'Ready when you are, Anthony,' he directed.

Braddock smiled. 'Great. So, just to say before we begin, that we weren't able to retrieve the two earlier pieces of footage. I'm afraid the recordings were wiped as per usual, given that they are a month old. But the footage from last week was available, and it's proven to be extremely helpful. Mike, if you please.'

Mike operated the controls and the footage played on the bank of screens in front of them. It was from the in-carriage ceiling mounted camera, and showed the man front on, standing close to a woman by the doors. The carriage was standing-room only, but not as busy as it could be down there. That was why it was possible to see the man's arm and hand, holding a mobile phone, angled underneath the woman's skirt.

Cullen and Marianne watched on. It was clear that this was a case of up-skirting, where an offender would use a device to take photos or videos underneath women's clothing. It was depressingly common on the London transport network, as it was too in other urban centres around the world with such huge numbers of people crammed together.

'So there is the offence,' Braddock said.

Cullen nodded. The fellow passenger who had recorded the incident and uploaded it to the MayDay app had been right in their suspicions.

'You can see how the lady doesn't realise what has happened,' Braddock continued, as they watched the footage and the man brought the phone back up, sliding it into his pocket. 'The train now enters the station, and our suspect alights.'

That was one explanation why the witness hadn't challenged what they had seen. By the time they had viewed what was happening, it was over, and the man was gone.

'So now we switch to the platform footage,' Braddock said. 'Mike here has made use of a number of cameras throughout the station, to track the suspect from train to the open air. It tells an interesting story.'

Cullen watched the man stride down the platform, past the camera, before the footage switched to a stairwell and then a tunnel leading up to ground level. The camera in the entrance hall captured him scanning through the barrier and exiting the station. The final footage was from an external camera, and showed the man making his way east away from the station before turning right and disappearing from view.

'We could get more footage of course,' Braddock said. 'I'm sure my friends at Transport for London would oblige, if I asked them nicely. We could then track him along the road for as long as we wanted.'

TfL, in charge of the capital's main transport network, had thousands of cameras throughout the city as part of their congestion and low emission zones. Although their main purpose was not intelligence gathering, the network had proven extremely useful for the Met, and on occasions the British Transport Police, as part of their investigations.

Cullen looked across at Marianne again, to check whether she had seen something he hadn't. She was staring straight at the paused screen, thinking, before noticing Cullen's gaze and turning to him.

'Anything?' Cullen asked.

She shook her head.

Braddock and Mike were looking at them both, like quiz-masters waiting for a correct answer.

'Shall we run it again?' Braddock suggested.

Cullen wanted another look. 'Yes, please.'

Cullen could have just asked him to put them out of their

misery, but he didn't want to be handed things on a plate. Call it policing pride, but he wanted to work things out for himself.

He knew Marianne felt the same way.

They watched the footage again. This time Cullen widened his scope of interest beyond their suspect. He scanned the fellow passengers on the train, on the platform, and along the stairs and tunnels towards the exit.

There was nothing particularly obvious.

'The man in the checked shirt,' Marianne tried. He's near the incident on the train, just a few feet away, by the door. And he alights at the station, is just behind Michael Gossage on the platform, and up the stairs towards the exit. I didn't see him in the final roadside shot though.'

Braddock smiled apologetically. 'Sorry,' he said, 'I thought that last bit might be too much of a giveaway. Mike, run the additional footage please.'

The extended roadside footage played and there was the man again, possibly tailing Michael Gossage along the road, and turning out of view at the same point.

'Could just be a co-incidence,' Cullen said, feeling somewhat deflated. He had expected more of a revelation than this, given Braddock's build up. 'The direction of travel, out of the station, and along the road, it's not exactly clear cut that this person was following our man.'

He looked at Braddock.

'Unless you've got something else,' Cullen wondered out loud as he continued to search Braddock for clues. 'Something from...the other footage?'

'But you said that's been erased,' Marianne said, directing her point between Braddock and Cullen.

'It has,' Braddock re-confirmed. 'But the public-generated

video clips you provided us with, they show something very interesting.'

Braddock nodded to his colleague, who pressed a button that brought up the first video.

Cullen and Marianne watched the video that both had already seen several times. It showed the man, once again standing in a relatively crowded carriage as with the more recent incident. This time he was directly behind a young girl. On this occasion, the mobile phone wasn't being used; instead, the man's right hand was positioned against the girl's bottom. It was done in a way that the girl didn't notice, but you could see the deliberate act that the witness had quite rightly identified.

'There on the right,' Marianne said. 'watching. That's the same guy, isn't it? The man in the checked shirt?'

Cullen had seen it too. 'Definitely.'

'Definitely,' Braddock agreed. And if you go to the other video, he's there again.'

They played the second video and there he was, just off to the left, again watching.

The video ended and Braddock waited for Cullen's response.

'They might have been working as a pair,' Cullen said, thinking things through. It did happen. Most of the perpetrators were lone wolves, but there had been instances where more than one person had been involved. These people often connected to others in online forums, and sometimes the relationships broke out of the internet into the real world.

'Like the recent case,' Marianne said.

Cullen looked across and nodded. They had recently arrested two young men who had been working with each other to target young girls on the tube.

Cullen played an idea around his head. 'Or...'

'We could be looking at the man's killer,' Marianne finished.

'Yes,' Cullen agreed. He looked at Braddock. 'Your thoughts, Anthony?'

Braddock opened out his palms. 'You're the detectives - I'm just the man with the cameras.'

'Oh you're much more than that, Anthony,' Cullen laughed. 'But fair enough, if you don't want to commit.'

This time it was Braddock who took the bait. 'If I was a detective, which as we've established I'm not, then I would say the latter is possibly more likely. I'd say you might have found your prime suspect in your murder investigation.'

'Mike?' Cullen asked, not wanting to leave anyone out.

'What the Boss says,' came the reply.

Cullen sat forward, thinking. 'So the big question is, who is he?'

# 17

*Tuesday afternoon*

DCI CULLEN and DI McGuire reached Lady Margaret's Academy, passing through the gates and making their way up the long drive. It was a classic 1960's build, which had recently been clad in bright blue.

They reported to reception and waited in a sofa area. The comfy chairs were so low down and soft that Cullen's knees were almost above the height of his head. He caught Marianne amused at the sight of him struggling to sit comfortably.

'Not sure they're built for people like you,' she noted, as Cullen gave up his struggle and decided to stand.

Cullen looked down at his colleague, perched expertly on the edge of the seat.

'I wasn't designed for sitting down,' he joked, brushing at his trousers. It was true. When he was a child, his parents had given him the nickname "Runaround", because of the fact that he never stood still. The nickname stuck and later on, during his rugby league career, it was all that he was known by - a tough, non-stop second row forward with a surprisingly agile side-step, and good turn of speed off the mark.

The name didn't however travel with him when he called time on his playing days and began his career with the British Transport Police - first up in Manchester, and then down in London.

He kind of missed the nickname. But then again, as age had begun to catch up with him in his mid-forties, he felt it probably wasn't as relevant anymore.

'Detectives?' a voice said as Cullen was inspecting the school notice board. He turned to see a well-built teacher heading for him, hand outstretched.

'Detective Chief Inspector Paul Cullen, British Transport Police,' Cullen said. The guy's grip was strong and was another reminder of his rugby days.

'Chris Barrington,' the man said, releasing his grip to turn to greet a now-standing DI McGuire.

'Detective Inspector Marianne McGuire,' she said, also taking his proffered hand.

'Pleased to meet you both,' the teacher replied. 'So,' he said, 'you want to talk to me about Michael.'

'Please,' Cullen said. 'Is there somewhere more private we can go?'

'Yes, yes, of course. We can go to my office,' he said, beckoning them to follow him. They moved along a carpeted corridor that was just off the reception, and followed him into a small office. 'This is what I get for being Head of Key Stage,' he said. 'Please do take a seat, officers.'

Cullen and Marianne watched as Chris Barrington picked up the pile of papers that were towering in the middle of the untidy desk and dumped them unceremoniously on top of the window sill. He turned back and scooped up the various other items on the desk's surface, cradling them into the corner of the room and placing them on the floor.

'Sorry,' he said. 'I've been meaning to tidy this place for a while, but, you know...anyway,' he continued, taking a seat, and looking between the two officers, 'how can I help?'

'We're trying to find out more about Michael Gossage's background,' Marianne began. 'In case there is anything that can shed light on what happened.'

'Yes, yes, he said. Anything I can do to help with this terrible situation. What would you like to know?'

'Maybe start with Poppy Jones,' Cullen replied.

Chris's surprise was evident. 'Jenny mentioned Poppy to you?'

'She said you'd warned her that Michael was getting too close to her.'

'I did,' he said, nodding. 'I hoped that she might be able to get through to him where I obviously hadn't.'

'So you'd raised the issue with Michael himself?' Marianne said.

'Oh yes, a number of times. They were the talk of the staff room, and more worryingly, in recent times the playground. But nothing I said made any difference.'

'So what was happening between them?' Cullen asked.

'To be honest, I don't think anything as such was happening. I think it was innocent - to an extent - but in teaching, it's not so much about the reality, but how things are perceived that's important.'

'Tell me about the situation,' Marianne said.

Chris shrugged. 'Michael was helping Poppy with her history studies. She'd been going through an extremely difficult time, her mum died from cancer last year, so she'd missed quite a bit of school. Michael offered to give her some catch up sessions, during breaks and then after school.'

'But people started talking,' Marianne said.

'Yes. Not at first. But you know what schools are like. Rumours, Chinese whispers...it can get dangerously hot very quickly if you don't extinguish the flames.'

Marianne looked up from her notes. 'And that's what you tried to do?'

'Yes. As a friend and colleague.'

'Why you? Why not the Headteacher?'

'The Head asked me to do it, because Chris and I are...were...good friends, and he didn't want things to escalate yet by going through a more official route. The Head likes to smooth things over if at all possible - it's just his way of doing things.'

'But Michael didn't respond to what you said?'

'I'm afraid not. He got quite angry actually, told me he wasn't doing anything wrong, that Poppy deserved his help after what she'd been through, and if people didn't like it, that was their problem.'

'So you went to his wife,' Marianne stated.

'On Saturday,' he said. 'I didn't do it lightly. Michael was furious after he found out. Called me on Sunday, after Jenny had spoken with him about it. Never seen him like that before. Calling me all the names under the sun, saying I was trying to ruin his marriage. But I wasn't sorry, because the alternative would have probably killed his career - the Head was ready to move in with a formal process. I told Jenny because I was trying to save Michael - he was a great teacher and a good friend.'

Cullen now entered the conversation. 'Michael disappeared that evening. You said he called you after his wife

Jenny had spoken to him. So that would be later on Sunday afternoon?'

'Yes, that's correct. Early evening - around six.'

'And that's the last you saw or heard from him?'

'Yes. I thought of going over there, actually, to try and smooth things over with them both. I didn't want to leave things the way they were - but then I decided it would be best to leave him to calm down and sleep on things. I thought we might get a chance to chat at school, first thing Monday.'

'Is there anything else that you think might be helpful for the investigation?' Cullen asked. 'Anything happen in the preceding week?'

Chris Barrington thought. 'Not really, apart from the fact that Michael went home ill on Friday. It was quite sudden - we were supposed to be meeting about some curriculum issues just before lunch, but he didn't turn up. When I checked with the office, they said he'd left.'

'Left the school premises?'

'Yes. He told the receptionist that he wasn't feeling very well.'

This was interesting. Jenny Gossage hadn't mentioned anything about her husband being ill on the Friday - which might have been an oversight rather than a deliberate omission. 'Did you try to contact him? Find out what was wrong?'

'I did try to call him a couple of times, but there was no reply. Then I got busy, and I sort of forgot about it.'

Cullen was thinking. 'Do you know if he saw Poppy that morning?'

'I'm afraid I don't know.'

'Do you think we might be able to speak to Poppy now?'

Chris blinked several times. 'Yes, I guess so. I'll have to find out what class she has.'

'That would be great,' Cullen said. 'Thank you. But only if she's happy to speak to us.'

'Of course,' Chris replied, frowning at some thought. 'So...do you think something at school might have some connection with his death?'

'Everything is possible until it's impossible,' was Cullen's reply.

# 18

*Tuesday afternoon*

'We need to tread carefully here,' Cullen said, as they waited in Chris Barrington's office for Poppy Jones to arrive.

'Totally,' Marianne agreed. 'Sounds like the poor girl has gone through a lot. First her mum dying and then her teacher.'

'Yes.' He thought about Michael Gossage. Maybe the relationship between him and Poppy was innocent, and it was just a case of a kind hearted teacher going that extra mile for a student in difficulty.

But his instincts told him otherwise.

Whether this had any connection to Michael's death though was a different question entirely.

*One step at a time...*

'Good idea of yours,' Marianne said, 'to let her bring a teacher of her choice into the discussion.'

Cullen had settled upon the idea before they'd arrived at

the school. It was the least they could do, to help Poppy through the experience.

She'd chosen Libby Taylor, an English teacher who Chris Barrington had explained was also Poppy's form tutor.

The door opened and Chris introduced Cullen and Marianne to Poppy and Miss Taylor. Poppy hardly looked at them, while Libby Taylor shook hands with both officers.

'I'll leave you to it then,' Chris said, pulling the door to.

The four of them settled in the confined space of the office. All eyes were on Poppy, while she looked down towards her lap.

'I'm really sorry that we have to do this,' Marianne began. 'We'll be as quick as we can.'

Cullen and Marianne had decided that Marianne would lead the questioning of the young, vulnerable girl. It felt like the right and sensible thing for him to back off and play the role of observer.

Libby turned to Poppy. 'It will be alright,' she said, placing a hand on the schoolgirl's shoulder.

Poppy nodded and for the first time looked up and engaged with the room.

She was an attractive girl, with deep brown eyes, a neat chestnut brown bob and lightly freckled skin. As she was a sixth former, she wasn't in uniform - instead wearing a jumper with jeans.

'What would you like to know?' she asked, her nervousness evident.

'How are you feeling?' Marianne replied, dodging the girl's question. They wouldn't start with the heavy questioning yet.

She shrugged. 'Okay.'

Cullen sat back, thinking that she looked anything but okay.

'I hear you and Mr Gossage worked closely together,' Marianne continued. 'His death must be upsetting for you.'

Poppy looked away briefly then back at DI McGuire. 'He was really good to me', she said. 'He helped me with my studies, went out of his way.'

'History, wasn't it?'

She nodded. 'Yes. I needed to catch up on my work, it was really stressing me out. I'd missed a lot of class, you see, because of my...well...my mum...'

'It's okay,' Marianne said. 'I'm really sorry to hear about your mum.'

Poppy nodded, as if she had heard this sort of comment a thousand times before.

'So Mr Gossage tutored you?'

'Yes. At lunchtimes. Sometimes after school.'

'For how long has he been tutoring you?'

'A few months.'

'Is Mr Gossage also your history teacher?'

'No.'

'But he offered to tutor you history, not your own history teacher...'

She shrugged. 'We got chatting one day in the sixth form centre. He asked me how my studies were going, and I told him I was struggling. That's when he offered to help me.'

'And did you know Mr Gossage before that? Had he taught you before?'

'No.'

Poppy caught Marianne glance at Cullen.

'Why? Is that important?'

'We're just trying to get a full picture,' Marianne explained gently. 'There's no need to worry.'

'Michael was a kind person,' Poppy said. 'Very kind.'

*Michael...*

Marianne paused, before deciding now was the time to probe a little deeper. 'I'm going to ask a few more questions, but if you're uncomfortable at all, want to take a break, then let us know. Miss Taylor can take you outside, no problem. But it's important that you answer as honestly as you can, Poppy. Is that okay with you?'

Poppy nodded, her eyes shifting to her form tutor and back.

Marianne moved cautiously ahead. 'Would you say that Mr Gossage and you were friends?'

Poppy looked uncomfortable at the question. 'Friends? Well...maybe...I think we were friends, yes.'

'Good friends?'

Her brow furrowed while she thought about something. 'Good friends...I...don't think so...I don't think.'

'But you were close? You'd spent a lot of time together over the past few months.'

'As teacher and student,' she replied back without missing a beat.

Marianne nodded, remembering what Cullen had said about the need to tread carefully, and deciding not to press her any more on that point.

'I know what people were saying about us,' Poppy said, picking up the vibe behind DI McGuire's questioning. 'I know people were talking about me and Michael.'

*There it was again.*

*Michael.*

'What were people saying?' Marianne asked, as innocently as she possibly could.

'People thought we were having an affair,' she stated. She looked at Miss Taylor. 'Even the teachers were talking about it.'

Libby Taylor reddened.

Poppy's face hardened. 'We were the talk of the school.'

'I'm sorry, Poppy,' Marianne said. 'But I'm going to have to ask this - was there any truth to the rumours?'

Poppy laughed in disbelief. 'I just knew it was going to be about this.'

Marianne felt they were about to lose Poppy's goodwill.

'It's not that we want to pry, but it's important for the investigation,' Marianne explained.

'You're looking in the wrong place,' she stated.

'I'm not sure what you mean, Poppy?'

Poppy straightened in her chair. 'Why don't you go and find out who killed Michael?'

'That's exactly what we're trying to do, Poppy.'

She shook her head. 'You're wasting your time.'

Poppy shook her head and sat there silently for a few seconds as the three adults watched on. She pinched tears from her eyes, and shook her head again. 'Please, just leave me alone.' She looked at her teacher. 'Please, Miss, can I go now?'

Marianne nodded to Miss Taylor, who without a word escorted Poppy out of the office.

'You made the right call,' Cullen said, once the door was closed. 'Best not to push her too much at this point. Plus we've got to weigh up the harms and benefits of this - I don't want to upset her unnecessarily if we're heading down a blind alley. Poor girl has obviously been through enough.'

Cullen couldn't help but reflect on his daughter's experiences again, and he recognised the torment in Poppy's eyes.

Marianne didn't reply, instead thinking deeply about something.

'You look pensive,' Cullen noted.

Marianne exhaled, and ran a hand across her face. 'There's more to this, Paul.'

'You think?'

'Definitely,' she replied.

'You think they were in a relationship?'

'Maybe. But something isn't right, I know that. Something went on between her and Michael.'

'How can you be so sure?'

Marianne looked away, struggling with something. 'Because,' she said, at last, 'I recognised the signs. She looked and behaved just like I did, when I was questioned about the man who had abused me.'

# 19

*Tuesday afternoon*

'My God, Marianne, I never knew,' Cullen said, as he looked on with profound sympathy at his colleague. They were still in Chris Barrington's office.

Marianne shrugged and smiled sadly. 'No-one knew. No-one apart from me and my abuser.'

Cullen shook his head. 'That's awful, Marianne, really awful. You don't have to tell me anything, you know. But if you want to...'

Marianne nodded. 'He was my athletics coach,' she began. 'When I was thirteen, in secondary school in Dublin, I was picked out for being a fast runner. I was invited to train in the city with a group of other girls, as part of a "School of Excellence" that the council had set up. They wanted to develop young female talent, with a view of representing the county and then hopefully country.'

Cullen just listened.

'The coach, Connor Fisher, he'd represented Ireland in the past. He was tall, dark and handsome, great smile, in his mid thirties. Still athletic. Us girls, we sort of worshipped him like a God. Everything was great at first, we were a close group, became really good friends. Connor trained us hard but it paid off, and I represented the county. I won my second race. Then my third. And my fourth. Connor started paying me particular attention - extra training sessions, coaching in psychology, and physio.'

'He assaulted you?' Cullen asked gently.

Marianne nodded ever so slightly. 'It was subtle. So subtle I didn't even notice it at first. You know what they say, about boiling a frog? If you do it gradually, the frog doesn't notice, until it's too late? That's how it was with me and Connor.'

'Can I ask what he did? You don't need to tell me if you don't want to.'

'He groomed me,' she replied, almost seeming amused by the fact. 'He made me feel special - wanted - and slowly but surely he normalised a situation that really wasn't normal, when I looked back on it. It started with conversations, then friendly touches, on the shoulder at first, fleeting, then more lingering on other parts of my body. Hugs after a good run. A kiss on the cheek in private. And then on the lips. It was just after I turned fourteen that he invited me to his house and slipped his hand down my pants.'

'DEAR GOD…' Cullen was sickened by Marianne's story.

'And I let him do it,' she revealed. 'I let him do what he wanted. I let him do it and I left the house, feeling...dirty. And like it was my fault.'

'But it really wasn't.'

'I know that now. But it took a long time to rid myself of those feelings that I had done something wrong. The shame, it lingers and festers, and eats into your insides.'

'I'm so sorry,' was all Cullen could think to say. Many times in his career he had been repulsed by the things that men had done to women and girls, and as he was now, often felt that sense of collective male guilt.

'It's okay,' she said. 'I got through it, eventually. And I wouldn't be sitting here today if that man hadn't done what he did. At eighteen I decided that I wanted to join the force, and try my damned hardest to help protect others from evil men like Connor Fisher.'

Cullen thought back to what Marianne had said at the beginning of the conversation. 'And you never told anyone about him?'

She closed her eyes briefly. 'I really regret that. After he'd assaulted me, I quit the club, quit running, and my parents got suspicious. They actually asked me if anything like that had happened to me - they'd watched a programme about a gymnastics coach who had abused young girls. But when they asked me, I denied anything had happened. The stupid thing was, part of me still wanted to protect him. Can you believe it?'

'I can, Marianne.'

'That conversation, in the following years, it bothered me almost as much as the abuse - how I could defend my abuser. So when I saw Poppy just then, her behaviour, her words, I knew that she was lying. I know that something happened between her and Michael Gossage. It may well not be connected to his death, but something did happen and she needs our help.'

'So what do you suggest?' Cullen said, conscious that given what Marianne had just revealed, Poppy wasn't the only person who might need help.

'I agree we shouldn't push her,' she said. 'But I'd like to talk to her again soon. Maybe tomorrow. On my own, if at all possible. I don't think we'll get anything from her otherwise.'

Cullen nodded. 'We'll ask the school before we leave. Probably still best to go through them.'

'Agreed.'

'What happened to Connor Fisher? Maybe it's not too late,' Cullen said, unable to switch off his desire to see justice prevail.

'He's dead,' Marianne stated. 'Committed suicide in his prison cell, just after he'd been arrested on charges of sexual assault.'

'So...'

She smiled tightly. 'Other girls came forward,' she said. 'Years after it happened to me. He'd been abusing others, for years. If I'd told the truth back then, I could have put a stop to it.'

'Just remember,' Cullen said. 'You're the victim here.'

'Not any more,' she replied defiantly.

# 20

*Tuesday afternoon*

Shazney was finishing off the nails of a customer when the door to the salon rang. She looked up, still fearful that it might be Carlton paying her another visit. But she calmed instantly when she saw it was Harvey.

He sometimes popped in to see his cousin, Harmony. They were very close - more like brother and sister.

'Shaz,' he said, using her nickname. 'Are you going to be free in a few minutes? I'd just like a bit of a chat.'

'I've got Tara coming in next,' Shazney said apologetically. 'We're full to bursting with clients today.'

'I'll take Tara,' Harmony said, appearing from the back, as if she had been waiting for the cue.

'Oh,' Shazney said, surprised and confused by the turn of events. 'Are you sure?'

'Certain,' Harmony replied. 'You go with Harvey. I'll deal

with Tara and by the time we're finished, I'm sure you'll be back.'

'She sure will,' Harvey confirmed.

Shazney looked between the two, suspicious about what this obviously pre-planned action was about.

Then her heart sank.

*Did Harvey know about her lie?*

She suddenly wanted to run away. But instead she focussed on finishing the consultation, taking each of the remaining nails in turn, until it was over.

Harvey was waiting for her on the sofa in the corner, on his phone, and he smiled when she approached after the customer had left.

They passed Tara at the door on the way out, who gave Shazney a confused look. Shazney heard Harmony begin to explain the change of plan to her just before the door closed.

'We can go to the cafe next door, if that's okay?' Harvey said.

'Sure.'

They ordered a couple of coffees and took a seat in the far corner.

'I expect you're wonderin' what this is about,' Harvey said, his serious tone setting Shazney's nerves on edge.

'Yes,' she replied nervously.

Harvey steeled himself, before being interrupted by the arrival of the drinks. 'Thank you,' he said to the assistant, taking a steadying sip of his black coffee. 'I hope you don't think I'm stickin' my nose in where it's not wanted, but I didn't think I had a choice.'

'A choice about what?'

'To tell you what I heard about your dad, and Carlton.'

Shazney was relieved that it wasn't about her dark secret,

but horrified about what revelation was to come. 'My dad and Carlton?'

'I've been hearing rumours,' he said. 'That your dad has asked Carlton and his group to take revenge on the police officer who chased Tyrone.'

'No.' The revelation shook her to her foundations. Her father had promised. He had sworn to her face that he wouldn't have dealings with Carlton and his kind.

Harvey looked sympathetic and uncomfortable at relaying the details. 'I'd heard it from a few people, around the neighbourhood. I thought at first it might just be the usual talk, or Carlton just biggin' himself up, but I decided to do some investigatin'.'

'Yes...?'

'As you know, before I turned things around, I used to be involved with people, you know? I've still got contacts if I need them, although I really don't like to go there any more. But I decided we needed to know, so I asked around, and I'm really sorry, but they confirmed the rumours.' He noted Shazney's reaction. 'I'm really sorry, Shaz, to have to tell you this. But I don't want your dad to get in trouble.'

Shazney's head was still spinning at the thought that not only had her father lied to her face, but that he was working with Carlton, giving him his blessing to commit more acts of violence. 'I can't really believe this,' was all that she managed in response.

Harvey nodded in sympathy. 'Your father is a good man,' he said. 'Everyone knows that.'

'Not any more,' she found herself saying.

'No, Shaz, he is a good man. He's just messed up right now, not thinkin' straight.'

'But why is he doing this? For me?' Shazney couldn't understand why her father would suddenly take such radical action. Yes, he knew that she was distraught by what had happened to Tyrone, but to do this, it didn't sound like him at all.

*And what good could it possibly do?*

'There's somethin' you don't know about your dad and Tyrone,' Harvey said. 'Somethin' that could explain what he's doing.'

'What?'

'You know he was dead set against you dating him?'

'Understatement of the century.'

'Well when you didn't break it off, he came to me, asked my advice about how he could try and help Tyrone escape from his situation. He knew I'd got out, escaped the criminality, so he thought I could help.'

'He tried to help Tyrone?' Shazney could hardly believe it. As far as she had understood, her father had been steadfast in his determination to have very little to do with his daughter's wayward boyfriend. 'What did he do?'

'Well I told him I wasn't sure anything was going to help. You know, I tried the same while Tyrone was dating my sister, Rochelle. Never did any good. But your dad, he wanted to give things a go - thought that if Tyrone had that father figure, it might make the difference.'

That would make sense. Her dad placed fatherhood as the most noblest of positions that a man could hold, and had told Shazney more than once that his proudest achievement was being a good dad. But she couldn't quite believe he would go that far with Tyrone. 'So he tried to be a father figure for him?'

'Yes,' Harvey confirmed. 'I know it's hard to believe,' he

said, seeing her reaction. 'He didn't want you to know, thought you might get upset and think he was interfering.'

'Actually I think it's amazing,' she replied, still trying to imagine her dad engaging with Tyrone in that way. 'Tyrone never said anything to me, either.'

'I guess it was between themselves. They went out for drinks together, also to see the football a couple of times.'

'This is so weird.' She smiled with happiness, for that moment forgetting that Tyrone was no longer here. 'It didn't work though,' she said, now back in her painful present. 'He couldn't make the difference.'

'He tried,' Harvey said. 'I think he was making a difference. But it was difficult to extricate Tyrone from Carlton and the others. A couple of times, he thought he'd done it, but they always found a way to lure him back in.'

'He did really try...' she mused.

'I think that's why Tyrone's death has affected him so much. He'd expended a lot of emotion. So what he's doing, although it seems terrible, it's understandable.'

'But it's not him,' Shazney said. 'These plans for revenge, it's not him.'

'That's why we need to help. We can't let this happen.'

'But how...what can we do?'

'We talk to him.'

'I've tried that,' Shazney dismissed. 'He lied to my face, Harvey. I believed him, but he lied to me.'

'Well we try again,' he said defiantly. 'I'll be with you this time. We have to make him listen. We need to convince him to call off whatever he's asked Carlton to do.'

'How do you know it will work?'

'I don't.'

'What about Carlton? If he finds out that you're interfering? You know how dangerous they are.'

'I'll take the chance.'

'You don't need to do this, you know.'

'Yes I do, Shaz. Look, I'm only where I am today because people believed in me. They gave me a second, third, fourth chance, and they really put themselves on the line for me, even put themselves in danger. We're not going to let your dad get dragged under.'

'Thank you, Harvey. Thank you so much.'

# PART III

# 21

*Wednesday morning*

'DETECTIVE CHIEF INSPECTOR CULLEN,' Krishna Chatterjee said, rising from his seat. He pumped his hand. 'Pleased to see you again, in better circumstances.'

Krishna looked dressed for a high-powered business meeting, wearing a dark three piece suit complete with cuffed open collar white shirt.

'Better for you, maybe,' Cullen said, as their handshake finally ended, 'but just another day for me.'

The last time Cullen had faced this man, it had been in a bedroom at New House, during his unofficial investigation into Natalie Long's disappearance. Krishna had been an early suspect, given his strange behaviour during his stay there.

Now Cullen was hoping that Krishna might be able to provide help in this latest case, bypassing the odious Sir Kenneth New.

'Yes, yes, of course,' Krishna said, apologetically. 'Please, detective, do take a seat and enjoy the view. Drink?'

Cullen looked at the comically large blue cocktail that Krishna had in front of him. It even had a mini umbrella and something on a stick, maybe an olive.

'Just a water for me,' he said, as the waiter hovered.

'Have you been up here before?' Krishna asked, as the waiter moved away.

'Yes,' Cullen replied, as he looked out across the London skyline towards The Shard from their elevated vantage point from the cocktail bar in London's Sky Garden, located at the top of the Walkie Talkie building. 'My daughter took me up here last year for my birthday.'

'Good, good,' Krishna said, obviously disappointed that he hadn't given Cullen his first taste of the experience. 'This is one of my favourite places to do business. It's like being on top of the world.'

Cullen remembered Krishna as someone who believed he was above others, and Sir Kenneth's comments about him had reinforced that view. It came as no surprise therefore that he enjoyed such elevated surroundings.

'I was really pleased to hear that Natalie was found safe and well,' Krishna said. 'Really relieved. You know, I felt terrible about how I behaved in the house. On reflection, it really wasn't a good move on my part to write that note, try to scare her off the way I did. It wasn't fair tactics.'

Krishna's poison pen letter, slipped under Natalie's bedroom door, warning her to leave, had placed him squarely in the frame when she had disappeared.

'I mean, you've got to understand, Detective,' Krishna continued, 'the pressure that I was under during that time. I can handle pressure, I really can, but sometimes, you know, it leads one to certain actions that, possibly, aren't ideal.'

He sipped at his over-sized bright blue cocktail as the waiter brought Cullen his glass of mineral water.

'That's in the past now,' Cullen said.

'Maybe,' was Krishna's surprising reply as he played with the umbrella in his drink. 'You know, Detective, those events, in the house, for me, they are very significant - very significant indeed.'

Cullen had no idea what he was talking about, but hoped it might lead to where he wanted things to go.

'I went into that house believing whole-heartedly that my future was with Sir Kenneth. He said I was a vital part of the future of Brand New, and I believed him - I trusted him. But the truth is, he used me, Detective. And he's still using me now. Or at least he thinks he is.'

'I don't understand,' Cullen said, although he thought that he did.

'I made my ambitions, my dreams clear to Sir Kenneth,' he said. 'I am straight talking, Detective, and single-minded in my ambitions. I knew what I wanted, and what I deserved. And I fully believe I had done all that had been asked of me to progress towards my destiny.'

'Your destiny?'

'Of becoming the heir to Sir Kenneth's business empire.'

Cullen blinked.

'You look surprised, Detective?' Krishna commented. 'But if you knew the story, you would understand. You see, these past few years, it has been my vision, my creativity, my intellect, that has taken the company forward. The apps, Vicinity, and now, MayDay, they are all mine. And yet he takes the credit. I thought I would be rewarded, but I'm afraid I came to realise that Sir Kenneth wants to keep me firmly in the shade.'

'I'm sorry to hear that,' Cullen said, playing along. 'I can see how that would be frustrating.'

'Exactly!' he said, clicking into a finger point. 'You understand.'

'I do.'

'How would you like it if you solved a crime only for someone else to take all the glory, stop you from fulfilling your true potential?'

'Furious,' Cullen said.

'Of course you would be. And that's how I feel. Except for me, it's worse, because I have so much more to give.'

Cullen resisted an eyebrow raise. Krishna was really a piece of work.

Instead he chose the moment.

'That's exactly why I want to speak to you, because I need your help...your vast expertise.'

'Go on,' Krishna said, immediately interested.

'Your creation, MayDay, it might be able to help me solve an ongoing case.'

Krishna leant forward. 'Yes...'

Cullen brought out his phone and swiped through to the set of video stills showing the unidentified man who had been seen watching Michael Gossage on the tube.

'I'm looking to identify this individual,' Cullen explained. 'They are a person of interest in an active murder investigation. This man here, Michael Gossage, was found dead on Monday morning on the tracks just outside London. The person I'm looking to identify was seen in his close vicinity on the underground network on three separate occasions.' He swiped through the images. 'Here, here, and here.'

'Interesting,' Krishna said, excited. 'May I?' he said, taking the phone off him. He scrutinised the photographs. 'These images, how did you get them?'

'From your MayDay app.'

He looked confused. 'Sir Kenneth gave you these?'

'Yes.'

His face darkened into a frown. 'I didn't know anything about this,' he said.

'He contacted me, saying he could help with the case, and provided me with three video clips that identified Michael Gossage.'

Krishna shook his head in anger. He looked up at Cullen. 'I didn't know anything about this,' he repeated. 'He's cutting me out.'

'I assumed...'

'No,' he jumped in, 'he deliberately by-passed me.' Krishna was thinking. 'He must have contacted Noel, my junior, gone through him, to run the analysis of the database. Yes, it had to be Noel.' There was another shake of the head. 'You know, Detective, why Sir Kenneth is so keen to take credit for MayDay?'

Cullen was pretty sure why. 'No.'

'To try and save his reputation,' Krishna said. 'All those people who have come forward, with their stories of what he did to them, he's scared of losing everything. For him, MayDay is a lifeline, to whitewash his past, to paint himself as the protector of women, the protector of London, when in fact the truth is, he's anything but. Do you know that a couple of weeks ago, he met the Mayor, to discuss the use of MayDay by the police across London?'

Cullen thought back to what Maggie Ferguson had said to

him about the Mayor's newly found enthusiasm for tech-led policing. 'No. But I'm not surprised.'

'He didn't invite me, of course. I didn't even find out until after the event, even though MayDay is my brainchild. And that's why I have decided to leave the company, to strike out on my own and follow my dream.'

'Good for you,' Cullen said, keen to stroke his ego if it got the results he wanted.

'Sir Kenneth is making himself out to be a saviour,' Krishna said, 'but the truth is, he's dangerous and he's going to get what he deserves.'

'That will be for the courts to decide,' Cullen said, keen to keep the conversation focussed and away from anything that could be seen to jeopardise the legal process - there was a limit to which he was willing to engage with this guy.

'Of course, of course,' Krishna nodded. 'I understand that you have procedure to follow, Detective. So,' he said, handing the phone back to Cullen, 'what do you want me to help you with, specifically?'

Cullen thought he'd made that pretty clear but kept his tone even. 'The identification of the person pictured with Michael Gossage.'

'I might not be able to identify him,' Krishna said. 'That isn't the aim of MayDay.'

'But...'

'The aim, first and foremost, is to provide immediate assistance to people in trouble - enabling them to call upon persons nearby to intervene in uncomfortable, even dangerous situations. Hence the name, MayDay.'

'Yes, I understand,' Cullen replied, mildly irked by Krishna's faintly patronising spiel. 'However...'

'However, as you've discovered, Mayday has another,

secondary function - to assist evidence-gathering by enabling users to document possible offences, and offenders, through photo or video recordings. Then, through my sophisticated artificial intelligence and facial recognition technology, we are able to match offenders across our database and build up patterns of possible crimes. Which is how my team helped you to find your Michael Gossage. But,' he said pointedly, holding up a finger to emphasise the words, 'it is very much in Beta testing at the moment. And does not identify individuals as such - to try and do such a thing would open us up to huge risk of litigation. MayDay instead provides evidence for the authorities, for you Detective, to identify who these people are. We provide the faces, you provide the names.'

Cullen nodded his understanding.

'So you see, Detective,' Krishna said, open-palmed, 'why I can't answer that specific query.'

'I understand.'

'But, what I can help you with, is whether there are any more entries for this person in our system. That might then help you with your investigation, might it not?'

'It might, yes.'

Krishna smiled. 'In that case, Detective, let's get to work.'

Krishna reached down and pulled out a laptop onto the table.

'You can do this now?'

'Oh yes,' he said. 'Through a secure network I can access our database and perform the necessary searches. Now if you could send me through those three images, we can get down to business.'

# 22

*Wednesday morning*

CULLEN SENT the images of the mystery man through to Krishna, along with an image of Michael Gossage and photos he'd sourced of Jenny Gossage and Poppy Jones from their social media feeds, in case they were useful.

After visiting the bathroom, instead of returning straight back to the table, he headed down the stairs to the open air viewing platform to take a few minutes to think. The impressive view of the capital city sprawled out below and in front of him, as the cooling breeze at this altitude touched his face. He stepped closer to the edge, which was thankfully separated from him and the other people by a high glass screen.

Still, the vertiginous view was a little stomach turning, even if he couldn't resist the view.

Cullen turned his attention to the River Thames that snaked through the city. A tourist boat cruised past, while a police coastguard skimmed quickly across the waters.

This city was so full of life, and it still excited him. He missed the North West of England, particularly as Sarah was currently living up there, but he would miss this place if he ever moved back.

In one of those strange co-incidences of life, as his thoughts turned to his wife, she called through on the mobile.

'Sometimes I do wonder if you're a white witch,' he joked, without waiting for a hello.

'Maybe I am,' Sarah joked back. 'Let me guess, you were just thinking about me?'

'That's what I mean,' he smiled into the receiver. 'Witchery.'

'You'd better believe it.'

Cullen moved away from the crowds and back into the indoor area. 'How did the meeting go?'

Cullen had been worrying about the outcome of the meeting, with senior staff at Acorn House, about the increasing aggression shown by Philip.

'It went pretty well,' Sarah said.

'Thank goodness for that,' Cullen replied, hugely relieved.

'They said they'd keep things under review,' she explained. 'But they don't want to do anything drastic unless they really have to. They don't want Philip to leave, as they've seen real progress.'

'That's great,' Cullen said, as he gazed down on Tower Bridge below. 'I'm glad they're thinking about what's best for him.'

'Which is why I'm so keen that he stays in there,' Sarah said. 'I hate to think what might happen if he moves somewhere else.'

'Me too.'

'So how's the case?' she asked. 'Any further forward?'

'A little,' he said.

Sarah was too experienced to ask about any of the details. 'Well I hope it works out.'

'So do I,' he said, the topic of conversation reminding him that Krishna would be waiting for him in the restaurant.

But would Krishna be able to move this investigation on?

~

As Cullen returned to the table, Krishna looked up with what the detective interpreted as a glint of excitement in his eyes.

'Sorry for disappearing,' Cullen said, retaking a seat, 'had to take a phone call.'

'No problem, Detective,' Krishna beamed from over the top of his laptop, 'absolutely no problem. It took a little time to run the searches, at any rate.'

Cullen was keen to get down to business. 'Any success?'

Krishna nodded. 'Yes, indeed. I must admit, I wasn't one hundred percent confident that we would have a breakthrough. But I'm happy to report that I was wrong on that score. Very wrong indeed, Detective.'

Cullen tried to hide his impatience. 'I'm all ears.'

Krishna pulled his chair around to Cullen's side, and turned the laptop screen towards them both.

'This is your man, isn't it?' Krishna said.

Cullen gazed at the image of the man, who was in a seated position on a tube carriage. It certainly looked like his man. But Cullen wanted to be more certain.

'Can you zoom in on the image?'

'Of course,' Krishna said.

With a single tap, the man's face was enlarged, and Cullen nodded. 'It's definitely him.' He turned to Krishna, intrigued. 'Did someone report him via your app?'

'Not him, no. The man next to him was reported for racially abusing a schoolgirl.'

Krishna scrolled to the man's right, to reveal another man, wearing a baseball cap.

'The notes say that this incident was also reported to Transport for London,' Krishna revealed.

Cullen looked back at Krishna. 'So our guy, he wasn't involved in the incident?'

'The notes say that some passengers intervened,' Krishna replied. 'He might have been one of them. But other than that, no, he wasn't involved directly in the incident that was reported.'

'Pan back to the man, can you?' Cullen requested.

Krishna did as asked, and Cullen studied the image on the screen some more as Krishna looked on.

He remembered Krishna's look of excitement as he'd first approached the table.

'There's more, isn't there?' Cullen said. 'You've got more images of him?'

'No more images,' he stated. 'Just this one.'

'Then I'm not sure how this helps,' he said, his frustration growing. 'It doesn't give us anything...'

'It's not another image,' Krishna interrupted, 'it's what else is on this image. After I saw who his companion was, I used the time you were away to verify their identity - just a quick whizz around social media. And there's no doubt about it. No doubt at all, Detective.'

Krishna scrolled to the man's left as Cullen's eyes widened in surprise and excitement.

Sitting next to the man was Poppy Jones.

'The man with her,' Krishna said. 'The man who you are looking to identify, is Poppy's father.'

# 23

*Wednesday afternoon*

GARY JONES, Poppy's father, worked as a manager at an engineering firm. A quick call through to his employer had confirmed that he was at work. Cullen and Marianne, who had reconvened following the breakthrough by Krishna, reported to reception. They waited for him to arrive in a small meeting room that the receptionist directed them to.

'Officers,' Gary Jones said warily, as emerged through the doorway. He closed the door behind him. Cullen eyed him - there was no doubt that it was him pictured with Poppy on the tube train. He looked a little older though than in the social media photos that Krishna had furnished him with. Older than his age of mid-forties. Maybe he was just tired.

Maybe.

'Is everything alright?' Gary asked. 'It's not something with Poppy, is it?'

He looked between them anxiously.

'Poppy is fine, Mr Jones,' Cullen assured him. 'There's no need to worry.'

Although that wasn't quite true.

'Good, good,' Gary said, putting a hand to his chest. 'You got me going there. So what is it?' His anxiety returned. 'Was it something I did on the road? I was a bit distracted this morning on the way to work.'

'Nothing like that,' Marianne said. 'Please do take a seat.'

He did as he was told, looking nervous.

'I'm Detective Chief Inspector Paul Cullen of the British Transport Police. And this is my colleague, Detective Inspector Marianne McGuire.'

'Gary Jones,' he said, his mind obviously still whirring. 'The office told me that you wanted to speak to me. How can I help?'

'We're investigating the murder of Michael Gossage,' Cullen said, letting the sentence sink in as he watched for a reaction.

Gary blinked a couple of times. 'Poppy told me that you'd spoken to her yesterday,' he said finally. 'I was surprised.'

'Surprised?' Marianne said.

He turned to DI McGuire. 'Because I don't know why you think my daughter could help with this. What could she possibly help with?'

'We're exploring all avenues,' Cullen said. 'It came to our attention that Poppy and Michael Gossage had recently been spending time together, and there have been rumours at the school.'

Gary Jones remained silent.

Cullen moved to press him more deeply. 'Were you aware of these rumours, Mr Jones?'

'No...well, yes, from one of the parents. But Poppy promised me that it was all rubbish. She's been through a very tough time in the past few years, and she needed help with her studies. He'd offered to tutor her, to support her with her work.'

'So you didn't have any concerns about the arrangement?' Cullen asked.

He shrugged. 'No. No concerns. He's her teacher, he was offering support. She promised me that it was all about the studies. Yes, I was worried that people were gossiping about her at school. But Poppy seemed okay with it, she said it was just the usual playground talk.'

'There were concerns among the staff, too,' Marianne said. 'Not just students.'

'Well I didn't know that,' he said. 'No-one told me. If they had been that concerned, shouldn't they have spoken to me, as her father?'

'I would have hoped so,' Cullen admitted.

'But I trust my daughter,' Gary continued, 'when she told me it was all above board.'

Gary looked at the two officers again, as if wanting to confirm whether his answer was enough.

Cullen exchanged a brief glance with his partner, before they continued.

'Mr Jones,' Marianne said. 'Did you ever meet Michael Gossage?'

'No,' he replied. 'Not that I remember.' He seemed to be thinking carefully about it. 'I don't think he was one of Poppy's teachers, so no.'

'So you've never had contact with him?' Marianne sought to confirm.

This time the answer was more definite. 'No.'

Marianne waited a few beats before producing the images of Gary on the tube, alongside Michael Gossage.

Gary looked shocked. 'But where...how did you...?'

Marianne didn't answer his question. 'Can you confirm you are the person pictured here?'

'I didn't kill him,' he said, still looking at the images. 'I swear, I didn't kill him.'

'Time to take this to the station,' Cullen said.

THE NEAREST BRITISH Transport Police station was at Clapham. It was a small office, but had the required interview room for the more formal questioning that was required.

Cullen explained to Gary that he was not under arrest, but was under caution and helping with their enquiries. Gary, who was now waiting in an adjacent room, had agreed to comply.

'What's your gut feeling?' Marianne said, as they prepared for the interview in their airless, gunmetal grey painted cell of a room.

'Open minded at this point,' Cullen said, testing the recording equipment. 'Ask me again in a few minutes. You?'

'Same, really,' she said. 'There's definitely more to learn.'

'There always is,' Cullen smiled. 'Let's get this done.'

Gary was led through by one of the officers on duty and sat down opposite Cullen and Marianne. He looked awful - haunted and frightened. The wait between the conversation in his workplace and now had obviously not done him any good at all.

Which wasn't a bad thing, Cullen thought.

Some people stayed remarkably calm and collected

during questioning. They were, for the most part, the hardest to break down. While others began to crack open at the first stress-test, providing the police with what they needed. Gary seemed firmly in the latter camp.

Cullen started the recording and summarised the background information to the interview, as Gary Jones waited nervously. Cullen's summary included the murder investigation and the events and discussions that had led up to Gary Jones being brought in for further questioning.

'So, Mr Jones,' Marianne began, once Cullen was done. 'Thank you for agreeing to help us today with our enquiries. We'd like to continue with our discussion about the images on the train that were shown to you earlier. Can you confirm that they are of you.'

Again Marianne showed him the images.

'That's me,' Gary said solemnly. 'They're all of me.'

Marianne nodded. 'The images show you on a London Underground train, in the near vicinity of Michael Gossage. On more than one occasion. Given that you stated in our earlier discussion that you've had no connection with Mr Gossage, can you explain these images?'

'I didn't lie,' he said. 'I never had contact with him.'

'But that is you,' Marianne said.

'Yes, yes, that's me.' He ran a hand roughly through his thinning hair, scratching at the scalp.

'So you did have contact?'

'No.'

Marianne feigned frustration. 'Mr Jones, either you did or you didn't. And you know what they say about the camera, don't you?'

'I followed him,' Gary admitted, his eyes set straight on DI McGuire, before switching to Cullen. 'I followed the guy. I wanted to find out more about him, whether he could be trusted.'

Marianne leant in. 'So you followed him, around London?'

'He lives nearby. When I found out about the rumours, about Poppy and him, I spoke to Poppy. She said nothing was going on, and I wanted to believe her, but, you know, I wasn't sure. So I decided to try and find out more about the guy. I knew he lived locally - I'd seen him out and about - so one weekend, when I saw him, I followed him back to his house. And after that, on other days, I waited for him and followed him on the tube.'

'It seems like an odd thing to do,' Marianne commented.

'Yes, I suppose it was.'

'What was the purpose of following him like that?' Marianne asked. 'I mean, what were you hoping to achieve?'

He shrugged. 'I don't know, really. I was suspicious, about his intentions.'

Suddenly it began to make sense to Cullen. 'You were checking if he was meeting your daughter,' he interjected.

'Yes,' he said. 'Or other girls. I wanted to find out what he was really doing with Poppy, if it was as innocent as she was saying. And I wanted to see if there was any evidence that he was doing things with other girls.'

'And did you find any evidence?' Marianne asked. 'That he was meeting up with Poppy outside school?'

'No,' he confirmed, 'I didn't.'

'And what about other girls?' she tried.

'I didn't see him with any other girls,' he said.

'And there was nothing else that you saw when you were following him that concerned you?'

'No.'

'You didn't see him engaged in any suspicious behaviour during the journeys on the underground?'

Gary looked genuinely confused. 'No. Why? Should I have done?'

Cullen nodded at Marianne to reveal further information.

'The images that we have presented you with,' Marianne said, 'they're stills taken from videos that were uploaded by passengers to an app, to report and document possible sexual crimes.'

'Oh.'

'Did you not see any activity yourself?'

'No, no I didn't.'

'I can play through one of the videos,' Marianne said, opening up a laptop on the desk.

Gary watched the footage that showed Michael Gossage seemingly positioning his phone underneath the skirt of a fellow passenger.

'I didn't see that,' he maintained. 'How could I? I'm standing on the other side, I wouldn't have been able to see the phone...'

Cullen thought that too as he watched the video back. Although he had been close to the incident, close enough to be picked out from the footage, Gary Jones' view was restricted.

'There's this one too,' Marianne said, playing another video. 'Here you can see that Michael Gossage is up very close to the lady in the red jacket.'

'Again, I wouldn't have seen that,' Gary explained. 'I mean, it's subtle, isn't it? And I was standing on the wrong side to see. The person videoing, they were in the prime position.'

Gary seemed to sense that the two officers were in agreement about this.

'Why did you lie?' Marianne said, closing the lid of the laptop as she decided to move on.

'About what?'

'About your contact with Michael Gossage?'

He shrugged. 'I guess I was afraid.'

'Afraid of what?'

'Afraid of being blamed for his murder.'

'What makes you think you'd be blamed for his murder?'

'Well I'm here now, aren't I?'

It was hard to argue with his reasoning.

# 24

*Wednesday afternoon*

SHAZNEY AND HARVEY decided that there was no way they wanted to challenge her dad at the family home. So instead they waited outside the bus depot in Victoria and met him as he emerged from the end of his shift.

'Shazney? Harvey?' he said, surprised to see them. 'What are you doing here? My God,' he said, clutching at his chest. 'Your mother?'

'Mum's fine,' Shazney soothed. 'She's absolutely fine.'

'Oh, thank the Lord,' he said, looking to the heavens. 'So why are you...'

'We were hoping we could have a chat,' Harvey said. He glanced at Shazney.

'About you and Carlton,' his daughter finished.

Her father shook his head. 'I told you, Angel', he said, 'I do not have dealings with that man.' He seemed overly defensive, Shazney thought. 'I gave you my word. And yet you come here, accusing me again. And you, Harvey, you think this too?'

'I heard rumours,' Harvey said.

'Rumours?' he laughed. 'Rumours are rumours.'

Shazney had never seen her father like this. 'Daddy...'

'I've spoken to people,' Harvey added cautiously. 'People in the community. They said the rumours are true.'

He turned to Harvey, suddenly and shockingly angry, his nostrils flaring and finger in a point. 'You are speaking about me in the community?'

'Daddy,' Shazney tried again.

'You are talking to people, spreading your gossip and rumours?'

'Only with a few people,' Harvey replied, sheepishly.

'A few people,' he scoffed.

'Mr Powell, the last thing I wanna do is spread rumours and gossip,' Harvey said, trying to defuse the situation. 'We want to help.'

He shook his head. 'You lie in wait for me outside my workplace, ambush me and accuse me of all things, based on rumours and innuendo.'

Shazney didn't like how this was going. 'Daddy, we want to help you.'

He put up a hand. 'If you want to help me, then you will stop spreading these lies and mind your own business, both of you.'

'You are my business,' Shazney countered.

'Ha,' he said in a most uncharacteristic confrontational tone. 'Is that what you thought when I begged you not to date Tyrone? When your mother and I were so sick with worry that I begged you not to do it?'

Shazney looked away.

'No, you told me it was your business, your life, your decision,' he continued. 'So please, Angel, stop this now. And you too, Harvey. I thought better of you both.'

Shazney and Harvey backed down, as her father got onto the front foot.

'Now if you don't mind, I'm going to make my own way home,' he said. 'Tell your mother I may be a little late for dinner.'

Shazney could never remember a time when her father had been late for their evening meal.

As they watched him walk away, Shazney turned to Harvey.

'You see what I mean?' Shazney said, her heart breaking.

Harvey nodded. 'I've never seen your dad like that before,' he said. 'Makes me even more worried.'

'So what are we going to do now?' Shazney asked, tracking her father as he crossed the street and disappeared out of view without looking back.

'Time for Plan B,' he replied.

'Which is?'

'We go talk to Carlton.'

'You don't have to do this, you know?' Harvey said, as they rounded the corner, heading towards the basketball courts that Carlton and his crew often frequented.

'Neither do you,' Shazney replied. It was true, Harvey could step away from this and get on with his life.

He wasn't involved the way she was.

'I know, I know, but we've been through this,' he said. 'I

want to help. But I can do this alone if you like, I understand if you don't want to speak to Carlton.'

Shazney had worse things on her mind than Carlton. During the journey back from the bus depot, she'd been thinking again about admitting her lie about what she had said to the detective. And she had so very nearly told Harvey the truth.

*Of anyone, he would understand.*

*He would know what to do.*

*To make things better somehow.*

But she hadn't quite mustered up enough courage, so the secret had stayed locked inside, free to eat away at her from within.

'I want to hear what he has to say,' she replied, steeling herself for what would no doubt be another difficult encounter.

'Let's do this then,' Harvey said, with a reassuring pat of her arm. 'Hopefully we can sort this out before it goes too far.'

Shazney feared it already had.

# 25

*Wednesday afternoon*

Harvey had been tipped off that Carlton was at the basketball courts, so it was no surprise to see the gang there, congregating around one of the hoops. The court was opposite the housing estate from which many of Carlton's crew originated, and had been a base for them for years now.

'Ha! Ha!' Carlton shouted as he saw Shazney and Harvey approach. 'What have we here?'

'We'd like to have a chat,' Harvey said, as Carlton stood there surrounded by the eight other men, most of whom were still teenagers. Carlton always surrounded himself with younger recruits.

'Oh, would you? You'd like to have a chat?' he mocked. 'Well, what do you think, brothers? Should I have a chat?'

The group knew better than to answer - instead they just smirked their challenge at the two interlopers.

'Well,' Carlton continued, as Harvey and Shazney stood

their ground. 'I suppose I can manage a few minutes for your chat. Although time is money.' He smiled. 'Please, begin.'

'On our own,' Harvey said. 'Just you and us.'

Carlton looked peeved that he had to move, but eventually swaggered over before directing Shazney and Harvey out of the court and off to the side, away from the group.

'So what's this about?' he said, fronting up to Harvey. 'Better be good.'

'What did my dad ask you to do?' Shazney blurted out.

Carlton turned away from Harvey's face and smiled at Shazney. 'Didn't you ask your daddy?'

'He said he didn't ask you to do anything,' she replied.

Carlton opened his palms. 'Well there you go then,' he grinned. He began to head back to the court.

'We know he asked you to do something,' Harvey shouted. 'People have told me the rumours are true.' Carlton paused and turn back around, closing the ground between him and Harvey slowly and with menace.

Harvey didn't take a backward step. He had lived and survived in this world and was used to dealing with people like Carlton.

'You think you're better than the rest of us, Harvey, my man,' Carlton said, inches between their faces. "Cause you're doin' your degree, you think you're superior...'

'No,' Harvey replied.

'Oh I think you do,' Carlton smiled. He turned his attention to Shazney. 'He your knight in shinin' armour, Shaz?' He gestured at Harvey. 'Come to save the day. You know, maybe he's tryin' to move in on you, now that Tyrone has been flat-packed by the traffic.'

Shazney shook her head in disgust.

'Well, Shaz, you can do a lot better than old peabody Harvey here,' he said, grabbing at his crotch and jiggling the bulge under his trousers. 'You know what I'm sayin', girlfriend?'

He laughed hard at his own joke.

'Whatever my dad has asked you to do, please, say no,' she said, ignoring his provocation.

'No can do,' he replied.

'Please...' She didn't want to have to beg with this odious man, but couldn't see any other option.

'I've given my word, Shaz,' he explained with mock sincerity. 'I don't break my promises.'

'Com'on, Carlton,' Harvey tried.

Carlton maintained his focus on Shazney, putting up a finger to quieten Harvey. 'Your daddy has entrusted me with a very important mission - very important - and I said I would do it. So I am going to do it. I'm going to see that justice is done.'

'I lied,' Shazney said suddenly. 'I lied about what the police officer said.' She looked at Harvey, who obviously didn't know what on earth was going on. 'I did tell him that Tyrone had assaulted me. That's why he ran after him. So it's my fault, not the police officer's. There's no need for any of your justice.'

After a moment of realisation, Carlton's face erupted into laughter. 'Oh, man,' he said, slapping himself on the leg. 'This is a twist, man, this is a Netflix-style twist!'

Shazney looked at Harvey for direction.

'Let's just leave it here then,' Harvey said. 'There's no need to do anything more. No need for revenge.'

Carlton was still laughing. 'Just wait until I tell the guys,' he said. 'You crack me up, man.'

'It's not funny,' Shazney said, her voice breaking with anger and guilt. 'Tyrone is dead.'

'Yes, yes,' he said, calming down. 'You're right, Shaz, he is dead. Because of you.'

'Go to hell.'

'I already live in hell,' he replied, seemingly deadly serious. He gestured around the area. 'The flames burn brightly in this part of town and the devil is always busy.'

'Please, Carlton,' she tried again.

'It's too late,' he said. 'The wheels have been set in motion, and you know what, I'm really lookin' forward to doin' what I've been tasked to do. Please, Shaz, don't try and spoil things for me - let me have my fun.' He grinned his challenge.

'Let's go, Shazney,' Harvey announced, sounding defeated, or at least deciding on a tactical retreat. 'We've tried our best.'

Shazney nodded, sickness swelling in her stomach as she reflected on their failure to convince the man standing in front of them to change off his deadly course.

'I think we're done here,' Harvey added, by way of a goodbye.

They felt the heat of Carlton's stare as they walked away.

# 26

*Thursday morning*

DI McGuire reported to the school reception, this time without her senior colleague. Cullen was back at Headquarters, following up on the news from Danny that the initial analysis of Michael Gossage's phone and computer had revealed extensive activities, both viewing pornographic material and also videoing people on the tube network.

But still nothing that provided a breakthrough in the case.

Marianne settled into the sofa in the waiting area. She smiled at the recollection of how Paul Cullen had struggled in the seat. He was really one of the good guys. Kind and fair in a way that, unfortunately, many of her male colleagues did not only fail to live up to, but even worse, didn't even aspire to attain.

She loved the police service, and hadn't for a minute regretted joining. It had been everything she had hoped for, mostly. The stubborn chauvinistic culture aside, she had made some wonderful friends, both men and women.

But none with whom she had shared her secret.

*So why now? And why DCI Paul Cullen?*

Yes, a lot was down to context and timing. Poppy's apparent situation had resonated so strongly it had knocked her off balance, leaving her unusually vulnerable and needing to reach out to someone.

Paul Cullen had been there to be that person.

But it wasn't just that. Despite not really knowing him beyond their professional relationship, she trusted him completely. She didn't for a moment think that he would share her story with others. And she had no doubt that if she needed it, which she was sure she didn't, he would help her.

'Morning, Detective.' It was Libby Taylor, the teacher who had supported Poppy through yesterday's interview.

Marianne rose to greet her. 'Sorry to disrupt the school for a second day.'

'Oh, no problem,' the young, bright teacher smiled. 'School is all about disruptions, believe me.'

'I can imagine,' Marianne replied.

'Poppy is waiting outside,' Libby said. 'She said she'd prefer to meet in the open air, if that's okay. We have a playing field off to the right there, or there's the tennis courts. There won't be any kids on them, so it will be private enough.'

'Thanks, that's perfect,' Marianne said. It was a lovely morning, with clear blue skies, and a walk and talk sounded ideal as well as being potentially more effective at getting Poppy to relax and hopefully open up.

'Can I just ask something?' Libby said. 'I mean, you can tell me to go away if you like, but what's happening here? Do you think Poppy really had something to do with Michael's death?'

'We can't rule anything out at the moment,' was Marianne's stock, professional reply.

Libby nodded. 'I can't see how it could be. I mean, how could it be connected? Sorry,' she added, seeing DI McGuire's face. 'I'm being nosey. It's just that...'

'No, go on...'

'It's just that Poppy, I've been her form tutor for the last two years. Taught her English too. She's a lovely girl. No trouble. Works hard, is enthusiastic, popular with her classmates. She's been through a terrible time in the past twelve months with her mother dying. Absolutely awful. And it did affect her, it would affect anybody. She did withdraw a little. But all this talk about her and Michael, I never believed it.'

'Why?'

'Well, erm, I just didn't. You've got to understand, schools are unique places - they're their own world, particularly when it comes to gossip and rumours. You think the playground is where it all happens, but it's got nothing on the staffroom.'

'Did you know Michael Gossage well?'

'Pretty well, yes,' she said. 'As much as you can know a work colleague, I guess. We were on a few school trips together. He always came across as professional. Not someone who would have a...you know...relationship with a pupil.'

The teacher waited for a response.

'Libby, I appreciate what you're saying. But unfortunately you'd be surprised at what I see in this job - people who have very different public and private faces. Sometimes it's those you least believe are capable of it.'

Libby nodded to concede that fact.

'Before I speak with Poppy, can I just ask you a quick question? You probably won't know the answer, but it's worth a try.'

'Sure.'

'On Friday, before Michael Gossage left school at lunchtime, do you know if he spoke with Poppy?'

'Not face to face. Not here in school, anyway.'

Her answer was much more assured than she had expected, or dared to hope.

'Why so sure?'

'Because Poppy was off sick that day.'

# 27

*Thursday morning*

'Poppy, nice to see you again,' Marianne smiled as she approached the teenager. Marianne nodded a goodbye to Libby Thomas, who returned inside.

'Is it?' Poppy replied, waiting until her teacher was out of earshot.

'Fair point,' Marianne said. 'Not many people are happy to talk to me when I'm at work. They're either victims or villains,' Marianne said deliberately, 'and for the most part, neither are too keen to see me.'

Poppy didn't reply as Marianne watched for any reaction.

'Shall we go for a little walk? You can show me around the school.'

Poppy nodded and led the detective off across the playground, past the empty tennis courts and along a gravel path that ran out away from the school buildings and onto the fields that were located next to a wooded area.

'The older children tell the Year Sevens that an old man lives in the woods,' Poppy said. 'And watches, waiting for children to go in, before grabbing them.'

'We had stories like that when I was at school,' Marianne replied. 'The bogeyman is a timeless tale.'

'I really believed it,' Poppy said. 'It gave me nightmares. Then in Year 8 one of the older children, they told me it was a story made up by the teachers, to stop us going out of bounds during lunchtime and breaks.'

She stopped and turned to DI McGuire.

'That's when I realised that teachers lie.'

Marianne said nothing, but filed that potentially highly significant comment for future use.

'Why do you want to speak to me again?' Poppy said, restarting her slow walk as Marianne stepped in time.

'We just need to get all the information we can,' she responded.

'I told you everything yesterday.'

Marianne knew that it would be highly counterproductive to challenge that assertion. 'You're very brave, Poppy,' she said.

The teenager seemed surprised. 'Brave?'

'For getting through those very difficult times, with your mum.'

She shook her head and laughed. 'It's got nothing to do with being brave.'

'Don't underestimate yourself.'

Again a shake of the head. 'I didn't have a choice,' she said. 'I didn't ask for my mum to get cancer and die. I didn't volunteer to be the girl whose mother is dead. I just had to get on with it, deal with it.'

'Okay, sorry, Poppy.'

'It's fine,' she said. After waiting a few beats she continued. 'It's just, people think they know what it's like, but they don't, they really don't.'

Marianne nodded.

'My dad, he enrolled me in a support group, for children whose parents had died. I went a few times, met a lot of people, but even them, they didn't understand what it was like for me. They were going through similar things, yes, but they didn't totally understand, how could they?'

'I get where you're coming from,' Marianne said. 'We all have our own experiences. In my job, sometimes I just need to do the best I can, to understand.'

'You seem like a good person,' Poppy said. 'Even if you're just doing your job.'

That got a laugh from Marianne. 'Thanks, I think.'

They walked some more before Marianne restarted the conversation. 'Yesterday,' she began, 'I told someone something that I'd kept to myself for many years.'

Poppy's interest was piqued.

Marianne continued. 'When I was about your age, well a bit younger, someone took advantage of me, someone I trusted. I thought he was a friend, even though he was a lot older, and for a while I blamed myself for what happened. I even defended him, in my own mind and also to others. I let him get away with what he'd done, and it meant that he went on and did the same to others.'

Poppy said nothing, walking with her face turned away slightly.

'But after a while, I realised that it wasn't my fault. He'd taken advantage of me, and the situation. And yet, it was only yesterday that I felt ready to tell my story. Do you know why I finally told someone?'

Poppy shook her head without looking at Marianne.

'Because of you.'

Now Poppy did meet her eyes as the two stopped their walk.

'I don't understand...'

'I recognised myself in you,' Marianne said. 'I knew that what had happened to me, all those years ago, had also happened to you.'

Poppy was already in tears.

'You can tell me, Poppy,' Marianne said gently. 'You're right - no-one can truly understand another person's situation, but believe me, watching you in the office yesterday, I understood well enough.'

Poppy tried to sniff back her tears, and Marianne had to resist the temptation to put her arms around this vulnerable girl.

'I can help you,' Marianne said. 'Not just as a police officer, but as someone who has been through it.'

'I'm so stupid,' Poppy said at last, wiping her eyes with her sleeve as the tears continued to fall. 'I believed him, when he said he wanted to be with me.'

'Oh, Poppy,' Marianne said, moving to comfort her. 'I'm so...'

'Sorry?' she shouted, stepping away from the officer. 'Why are you sorry?' Another step back. 'I'm the one who was the idiot! I'm the one who believed his lies, let him do what he wanted, thought that we had a future. He said he loved me, not his wife! Do you know that? He said he loved me!' She turned in a slow, full circle, screaming at the sky.

Marianne tried to move in again, and this time, thankfully, Poppy let her.

'Come here,' she said, her arms around the stricken

teenager. She pulled her tighter, as if she was hugging her younger, former self. 'You did nothing wrong...'

'I did, I did,' she sobbed into her shoulder.

'Please, Poppy, don't blame yourself. Whatever he did to you, it isn't your fault. You don't have to say anything else, not yet, just remember that you're not alone, I'm here to support you.'

For a few long seconds they held one another.

Then Marianne thought she heard Poppy say something, but couldn't quite catch it. 'Sorry, I didn't quite hear...'

'I'm pregnant,' Poppy whispered, shaking slightly as she tried to stifle the sobs. 'I'm pregnant with his baby.'

# 28

*Thursday morning*

Cullen parked up outside Gary Jones' workplace and paced into the main reception. He'd set off there as soon as Marianne had called through with the news that Poppy was pregnant with Michael Gossage's baby. It may not have been the breakthrough it seemed, but it certainly provided a strong motive that required urgent investigation.

And Cullen's gut instinct was that this was a significant development.

This time, Cullen wouldn't give any prior warning of his arrival – the element of surprise and the shock it would bring might just knock Gary off balance enough to give Cullen the chance to find out the truth.

Marianne had remained at school with Poppy, making sure that she was okay. The poor girl had to suspect that her father could be in serious trouble, as much as they had tried to shield her from events. Now that they knew of the pregnancy, it was even more important to try and protect Poppy, but it could only be for so long and to a certain extent.

Unless of course Gary Jones and his daughter were innocent.

'Hi,' Cullen said. 'I'd like to speak to Gary Jones,' he said. It was a different receptionist than last time. She looked flustered, as if he'd caught her in the middle of a stressful situation. 'I'm Detective Chief Inspector Paul Cullen, British Transport Police.'

'But...' she began with surprise, 'I only called you a minute ago. How did you...?'

'I don't understand,' Cullen replied. 'I haven't had any...'

And then the realisation hit.

'What's happened?' he said with urgency.

'Gary Jones, he's up on the roof, he's threatening to jump.'

'Hell,' Cullen said.

*Had he been tipped off by Poppy?*

'Which way to the top?'

'Stairs are there,' she said, pointing towards the left. 'Or there's the lift...'

Cullen was already off. He barged through the double doors and powered up the steps two at a time. The building was four or five stories high, he wasn't sure exactly, but he kept going, pushing through the burn in his legs, until he reached the top.

He burst out into a corridor, where three people were in urgent discussion. Introducing himself with a quick flash of his ID badge, he moved past them and out onto the roof.

There was no time to lose.

# PART IV

# 29

*Thursday morning*

Malcolm Powell couldn't sleep. He tossed and turned, gripping onto the sheets like a parachutist in free-fall, while his wife slept soundly beside him. Turbulent thoughts battered his head, about the plans that were now well advanced and about to come to fruition.

*But what if something went wrong?*

It was the longest night, and he finally gave up at four in the morning, trudging downstairs and flicking on the television.

There was a re-run of a primetime quiz show, where contestants sought to battle against each other for a million pound prize.

The distraction worked, and he fell into a deep sleep, bolt upright in the armchair.

Waking with a start, disorientated and with a stiff neck, he realised he was now late for his morning shift. Skipping the shower, he dressed and ate quickly, and fled the house before his wife or daughter rose from their slumber.

He couldn't take any more questions.

How he hated lying to his beloved daughter.

It was time to finish it. Later that day, in between routes, he made the first call that marked the beginning of the end.

'I want you to do it tonight,' he said, his voice betraying his nerves. 'The person we agreed on, the police officer. The time we agreed on.'

His hand was shaking as he brought the phone down from his ear.

He blew out a long breath to try and steady himself, looking around to check again that no-one was in earshot.

And then he dialled.

'Hello,' he said. 'My name is Mr Malcolm Powell…'

# 30

*Thursday morning*

GARY JONES WAS SITTING on the ledge that ran around the flat roof of the building. He saw Cullen immediately, meeting his stare, before turning his gaze downwards towards the deadly drop.

'Gary,' Cullen said, voice calm and assured. He nodded at the only other person who was up on the roof, presumably one of his colleagues who had been trying without success to coax him inside. 'Police,' he said to the guy, who nodded.

'I'm going to do it!' Gary shouted, still looking down. 'I'm going to do it!'

'Please, Gary,' Cullen replied, taking some tentative steps forward. 'We can talk about this. Whatever the problem is, we can talk about it. It doesn't need to be like this.'

Gary looked over towards him. 'It's too late,' he shouted into the stiffening breeze.

'No, it's really not,' Cullen countered, continuing to close the gap between them, while being careful not to push things too far. 'I know it might feel like that at the moment, but it's never too late.'

Gary shook his head. 'I didn't mean things to turn out like this! I didn't mean to kill him.'

'Let's talk about this downstairs,' Cullen said, trying not to be too distracted by Gary's confession.

It seems like they had their murderer.

But this needed to be discussed in a police station, not on the roof of a building. There was no way he was going to let Gary Jones fall to his death.

'Why did she have to get caught up with that man?' Gary asked. 'She's a good kid, Poppy, she's always been so good. But that man took advantage of her.'

'I know he did,' Cullen agreed. 'It's not Poppy's fault.'

'I was a fool,' Gary spat. 'I thought it was innocent. I trusted him. But it wasn't innocent at all. He groomed her, abused her, used my daughter for his own sick pleasure. By the time I realised what was happening, it was too late, all too late. I let my wife and daughter down.'

Gary looked back over the edge and Cullen, still closing the gap, worried he just might jump, now he had admitted to this most serious of crimes.

'Poppy needs you,' Cullen tried. 'She really needs you now. More than ever.'

Gary shook his head. 'She needs someone who can really look after her.'

'I think you'll find Poppy wants you to be there,' Cullen said.

Gary let out a bitter laugh. 'But I won't be there for her, will I? I'll be in jail. How can I help her from behind bars? I'll just be an embarrassment to her.'

'Gary. Let's just take one thing at a time.'

Gary looked over again, with Cullen now only a few feet away. Not yet within touching distance, but close enough to now have a more discreet conversation and to maintain proper eye contact.

'I didn't mean to kill him,' Gary repeated, more calmly this time. He frowned at a thought. 'I told you, that some of the parents warned me about him and Poppy. I followed him, from his home, followed him around London. I did it a few times. I thought I might see him with Poppy, or another girl, but what I saw, it was worse than that.'

'Tell me...'

'I did see him doing those things on the underground,' he admitted. 'I saw him looking under girl's skirts, using his phone.' He shook his head at the memories. 'I saw him getting too close to people, women and girls, right up behind them. It was shocking...sickening.'

'I can imagine,' Cullen replied. This was all falling into place, but his primary concern here was to get Gary out of harm's way. It was a gamble to know whether engaging in this conversation would make a negative outcome more or less likely.

'One time,' Gary continued, 'I followed him to Soho, and saw him going into a building. It didn't have any signs outside, so I asked a few passers-by what was in there. They told me it was a brothel.' His face twisted in disgust. 'And this man was a teacher. A trusted person, working with children. Spending time alone with my child. How would you feel if it was your daughter?'

'Horrified,' Cullen replied with honesty. 'And angry.'

'You understand,' he said.

And to an extent, Cullen did understand. 'We can talk more later.'

'I want to tell you everything now,' Gary replied. 'Now that I've started.'

Cullen wasn't going to argue with him. If this was going to end well, it needed to be largely on Gary Jones' terms. Ultimately, only Gary could decide what the outcome from this high-risk situation would be. 'I'm still listening.'

'After the brothel, I felt I had more than enough to tell Poppy,' he continued. 'On Sunday evening, we'd had our tea and were sitting in front of the TV. I didn't know how to get the words out. And before I could tell her, she starting crying. That's when she told me.'

'About the baby?'

Gary nodded, his eyes closing at the memory. 'She told me she'd just found out, on Thursday, and that it was definitely his.' He put a hand to his head, finding it difficult to get the words out. 'She said they'd just done it the one time. At a hotel. She thought he loved her, but after she told him about the baby he didn't want anything to do with her and told her to get rid of it. God, it makes me feel sick.'

'Did you tell her about the others things he did?'

'No. What was the point? I just thought it would hurt her even more, to know what the father of her child was really like.'

'I understand.'

'She was adamant that she wanted to keep the baby. My poor girl, she was so broken, I just wanted to be there for her, to make things right. And to make sure he didn't get away with what he'd done.'

'You went to see him,' Cullen stated.

Gary nodded. 'Poppy didn't know, and she still doesn't.

That night, when she finally fell asleep, I went around to his house. I was going to tell everything, in front of his wife, and ruin his life like he's ruined Poppy's. But he was just leaving when I got there, so I followed him again, into the park across the road. I don't know what he was doing there, but I went right up to him, challenging him about Poppy, asking him what the hell he was playing at with my daughter. He wouldn't answer, tried to shrug me off, and we ended up fighting on the floor in the dark.'

Cullen just listened, simultaneously taking in what Gary was saying while also thinking about his next move.

*How long should he let the conversation continue for?*

*How much should he allow Gary to reveal, outside of the official police interview?*

'Gary. I think you would be better telling me the rest of this back at the station,' he said, deciding that this was the point to try and shut things down. 'With someone who can support you.' Maybe if he could convince him that the full story should be told elsewhere, it might decrease the likelihood that he would do something drastic up on the roof.

But Gary wasn't having any of it.

'He was fighting to get away - really struggling,' he said. I was on top of him, holding him down, trying to get him to listen. But the more he struggled, the more angry I felt, you know, that he didn't care about what had happened to Poppy, he just cared about himself. He caught me in the face, so I hit him back, a few times. I just couldn't stop. I hit him, and hit him, and hit him. It was automatic, I'd stopped thinking of what I was doing. I think I had him around the throat, squeezing, pressing down as hard as I could. And then I realised that he'd stopped moving.'

Gary looked at Cullen.

'I panicked,' he continued. 'I was going to leave him where he was, but then, I decided to move him. I hid him in the bushes, went back to get my work van, and then put him inside. That's when I decided to drive to the railway yard, and leave him there, on the tracks.'

'Why there?'

'I visit there with my work,' he revealed, 'we have a contract with the freight company. I thought if I left him there, late at night, he might, you know, get hit by a train, and then people would assume that's what had killed him. When I think about it now, it's a stupid idea, but I was panicking. I cleaned him up as best as I could, to remove fingerprints, and left him there.'

Gary gazed at Cullen for a reaction. 'I didn't mean to kill him,' he repeated.

'Let's get you down from here, mate,' Cullen replied, sensing that this was the moment to seize. He reached out a hand and Gary took it, stepping back over the ledge to safety. Cullen shepherded him across the roof.

'You're going to charge me with murder?' Gary asked, as they reached the door back down.

'Let's talk some more downstairs.'

Cullen wanted to make sure that Gary was okay before reading him his rights and making the arrest.

# 31

*Thursday afternoon*

CULLEN DROVE Gary Jones back to the police station where they had first questioned him. He didn't say anything more to him during the journey. The rest would wait until the interview, where Marianne would join him.

As Cullen travelled to their destination, he glanced back at Gary, who was staring blankly out of the window. He wondered what he would have done in the same position - would he too have felt the need for revenge on the man who had done such harm to his daughter?

Maybe.

But as understandable as Gary's actions had been, he had clearly gone too far, and would now have to pay the price.

Cullen parked up and led Gary through to the front desk before booking him in. The duty sergeant took over from there, taking Gary's details, before leading him to one of the holding cells.

'So you got a result then?' the sergeant said, returning from securing Gary in the cell.

'Yes,' Cullen replied. 'Looks like it.'

'You don't look so happy about it, if I may say,' he commented.

'No,' Cullen replied, 'I'm not....for some reason.'

'Well congratulations anyway,' the officer said. 'I'm sure you'll feel it later.'

He went back to his paperwork as Cullen paced slowly around the room, waiting for Marianne to arrive.

*Why did he feel that sense of deflation?*

*Was it because he empathised with Gary Jones that bit too much?*

*Or was there something else...*

*Something that was not quite right about all of this.*

'Paul,' he heard Marianne say, as he was lost in thought.

Cullen turned and smiled at his colleague. 'Marianne.'

'Congratulations,' she said.

'Is it?'

She looked incredulous. 'You simultaneously stopped a man from jumping to his death and solved a murder case. Not bad for a day's work, Detective Cullen.'

'Well when you put it like that,' he said, giving a troubled smile. His mind was still whirring with possibilities, working through problems that he had thought were resolved.

And yet...

'What's up?' Marianne asked, stepping closer to him. 'That look, you're not happy about something.'

'I'm not sure,' he replied.

And then it came to him, emerging from the mists of his mind.

The note.

'You don't think this is the end,' Marianne deduced correctly. She saw his reaction and her excitement grew. 'That's it, isn't it? You don't think this is everything.'

'It's just a thought,' he said.

'Your thoughts are usually correct,' she replied. 'Tell me.'

'How was Poppy, back at the house?' he asked.

Marianne shrugged. 'Better. Calmer now. But she's got a lot to deal with, what with the baby and now this with her father.'

'Did she ask about him?'

'No.'

'And yet she called him. To warn him that we knew about her pregnancy.'

Poppy had admitted as much, after they had checked Gary's call log.

Marianne nodded. 'You think she knows more about what happened?'

'Maybe,' he said, still thinking. 'You said Poppy's now with her neighbour?'

'Yes. Her neighbour and their daughter, who's a schoolfriend.'

'Good,' he said.

'So are you going to tell me what you're thinking?' she tried again.

'The note,' he said finally. 'The note we found on Michael Gossage. I don't think Gary Jones wrote it.'

ONCE MORE, Cullen and Marianne sat across from Gary Jones. This time, he had a solicitor for support, a pleasant, highly competent woman called Catherine Cox, whom Cullen had dealt with several times in the past.

Cullen outlined the background again for the recording, and they talked through the events again of how Michael Gossage had come to lose his life.

'So the events that you outlined to me earlier,' Cullen said, 'you maintain that this is what happened?'

Gary looked surprised at the question. 'Well, yes, of course, I've just told you.'

Cullen nodded. 'We just need to be sure,' he said. He held Gary's gaze. 'We need to be certain about exactly what happened.'

'Don't you believe me?' Gary asked. 'Why would I lie and admit to murder?'

You're lying, Cullen wanted to say to him. I can tell now that you're lying.

And he was sure Marianne would be thinking the same.

There were some truths there, for sure, but it wasn't the whole truth.

'You haven't mentioned the note,' Cullen said. He raised an eyebrow at Gary.

'The note?'

'Yes, the note.'

'I...' he looked at Catherine Cox. 'I don't know what you...'

Cullen was careful to choose his words carefully. Very soon, Gary would realise what was happening, and Cullen didn't want to ruin the opportunity.

'The note that was left with the body,' he said, finally.

Gary was trying to think on his feet, but Cullen could see the panic.

'Oh, the note,' he said, 'Yes, the note.'

Cullen waited a few beats. 'What was the purpose of it?'

'Well....I...I just wanted to...you know, leave...'

'Can you remind me, Gary, what the note said?'

'Yes...well....no...I can't remember.'

He looked at Cullen and Marianne in turn.

'I was panicking, I can't remember a lot about what I did, I know I wrote something, a note, but I can't remember what exactly.'

'So you're saying that you wrote the note?' Cullen pressed.

'Yes. Yes, I did.'

'And if we were to perform handwriting analysis on the note, it would match you?'

He frowned. 'Yes. Yes, it should...'

'Should?'

'It would, yes. Maybe it would be a bit different than normal, because of, you know, the panic, the situation...'

'Or would it match the handwriting of someone else?' Cullen tried.

Gary Jones looked sick.

Cullen took no pleasure in finishing this, but it had to be done. 'The handwriting of your daughter, Poppy?'

Gary shook his head. 'No...no.'

'We *will* do the analysis, Gary,' Cullen warned. 'Better to tell us now, than to wait for the results to come back.' The warning was heartfelt - he didn't want this guy to dig himself any deeper, and risk more difficulties in the coming court case.

Gary began to sob, both hands cupping his shaking face.

Cullen waited.

'Please,' Gary said, through his hands. 'Please, she's just a child. My little girl. She'll have her own baby to look after.' He took his hands away to face Cullen, man to man, father to father. 'Please, Poppy doesn't deserve this. My beautiful daughter. She's a victim.'

Cullen felt a lump in his throat. 'I know,' he said, taking no comfort at all that his instincts had been right. 'I know she is.'

# 32

*Thursday afternoon*

DI McGuire approached the house of Poppy's neighbour, Sally Speed, still feeling sick from the realisation just twenty minutes ago that Poppy bore at least some responsibility for the death of Michael Gossage.

She felt so sorry for Poppy, no doubt because her situation resonated so strongly with her own. They had both been abused by men in whom they had put their trust.

One of them had run away, tried to bury the horror.

The other girl had seemingly fought back and defended herself.

*Who had done the right thing?*

Running away had allowed her abuser to get away with his crimes for several more years, and had exposed other vulnerable young girls to his vile actions.

She paused in a knocking position as she thought that through.

What if she had taken matters into her own hands, those years ago?

Others would have been spared.

But where would she be now?

Finally knocking, she waited until Sally, the lady who she had left Poppy with, answered.

'Oh, Detective, hi,' she said, obviously surprised to see her back so soon. 'Come in, please.'

Marianne followed her through into the living room.

'The girls are upstairs,' she explained. 'Would you like me to go and get Poppy?'

'Yes, please,' she said.

Sally went to fetch her, but then paused by the door and turned back towards Marianne. 'Is everything okay, with Gary, with Poppy's dad?'

'He's fine,' Marianne said. 'He's with my colleague, down at the station.'

Sally nodded, troubled. 'This is about the death of that teacher, isn't it, Mr Gossage?'

'Yes.'

'You think that Gary Jones...'

'Mrs Speed...' Marianne cautioned.

Her face darkened. 'You think...Poppy had something to do with it?'

'I really need to speak with Poppy,' Marianne insisted.

'I know about the baby,' she said. 'And I know whose it is. Poppy told us both while you were out. It's all just so, so terrible. What that man did to her, it's awful.'

'I couldn't agree more,' Marianne wasn't afraid to admit.

'I mean, she's a lovely girl. Known her since she was a baby. She's been friends with my daughter Matilda since they were crawling. A kind, bright girl.'

Marianne nodded. 'I can tell. Sometimes good people end up in bad situations.' The comment wasn't meant to be flippant, it just reflected the fact that in her policing career, Marianne had seen it many times before - too many times.

Crime and criminality weren't reserved for career criminals. It could touch the lives of anyone and sometimes it blew their world apart.

'If it had been my daughter that he'd done that to, I would have killed him myself,' Mrs Speed stated, deadly serious.

Marianne was fast losing patience - Sally Speed really didn't have any idea of the nightmare that Poppy and Gary now found themselves in, the awful reality of it all, lives changed forever. 'Mrs Speed, please, can you go and get Poppy.'

~

THE MOMENT that Marianne came face to face with Poppy, she knew that the young girl was ready to confess.

As with Cullen earlier, there was no sense of euphoria about this. It was the hardest of cases, where the roles of victim and villain were not just unclear, but felt reversed.

'You want to take me to the police station?' Poppy asked, as she stood in the doorway, shoulders slumped and face drawn.

'Not yet,' Marianne replied. 'We can talk here first, if you like.'

Poppy took a seat and Marianne asked Mrs Speed if she would like to remain in the room, for support, which she did. Poppy's friend Matilda had also come downstairs, but was ushered back up with some resistance by her mother.

'Before we begin, I need to caution you,' Marianne explained, taking no pleasure in any of this.

'How did you know?' Poppy asked, blinking away tears, after Marianne had read out the standard caution.

'The note,' Marianne replied.

'The note,' she said, thinking it through. 'He had the note in his hand, when he came out of the door - he must have put it in his pocket. I didn't think.' She nodded, satisfied with the explanation, then met Marianne's gaze. 'I knew my dad wouldn't have told you.'

'Your dad said that he was alone on the night that Michael Gossage died. But that's not true, is it, Poppy?'

'No,' she said.

'Can you tell me what happened?'

She nodded. 'I was so mad, that night, Sunday evening. So angry, and hurt. It was like I was in another place, you know, in my mind...after what he'd done. But you've got to believe me, that I didn't mean to do it, I just wanted, you know, him to suffer for what he'd done to me. And to the other girls.'

So she *did* know about Michael Gossage's wider behaviour...

'When I first met Michael, he seemed so kind. He'd never taught me, but I'd seen him around and heard from my friends in the school that he was a really good teacher. The day he approached me in the sixth form centre, he was so friendly and offered to help with my studies. He knew that I'd been struggling with things since my mum...you know...since my mum died.'

'So that's the first time you ever spoke to him?'

'Yes. As far as I can remember.'

'What did he offer to do for you?'

'Like I said, help with my studies. Just at lunchtime for quite a while. It really helped me. I caught up with my work, and then overtook some people in the class. I was really enjoying it, talking and learning about the subject with him. I know it sounds a bit sad, but he made it seem exciting. He wasn't like the other teachers...'

Marianne could imagine the scenario now, the two getting closer as the boundaries between teacher and pupil, adult and child, blurred - or more accurately, were carefully and deliberately erased by Michael Gossage. 'Was it only at lunchtime that you met with him?' she asked, knowing already from others that the answer was no.

'We started to meet after school - at school. Then we met outside school too, at a local cafe. We also met on a weekend too. At a hotel.'

'A hotel?'

'Yes,' she answered, more hesitantly. 'In the day, a few weeks ago. He booked a room, at a hotel in the centre of London. Said that it would be an ideal place to do some studying, because we wouldn't be disturbed and there was a desk in the room.'

And a bed, Marianne thought.

'That's not where it happened,' she said, reading the detective's thoughts. 'Nothing happened that day.'

Marinane nodded.

Poppy smiled sadly. 'He said that he loved me. That he didn't want to be with his wife; he'd rather spend time with me. And I believed him. What an idiot.'

'Don't blame yourself, Poppy,' Marianne said. 'You mustn't.'

'You're going to blame me for killing him though, aren't

you?' she shot back. 'I need to take responsibility for everything I've done.'

'Tell me what happened, Poppy. I can't promise anything, but I will do my best to support you through this.'

'Why? Why would you want to help me?'

'Because I understand what you've been through. We were both taken advantage of, abused, forced to make decisions to get it to stop.'

She shook her head. 'You became a police officer. I became a murderer.'

'I ran. You fought back,' Marianne said. She regretted her words immediately. No matter how much she empathised and cared about Poppy and her situation, she was getting too involved emotionally and her comment was not only inappropriate but unprofessional. Maybe she should have let Paul Cullen do this. She gathered herself. 'Sorry,' she said. 'If you don't mind Poppy, we need to do the rest of this properly, down at the station.'

# 33

*Thursday afternoon*

'ARE YOU OKAY, SHAZ?' Harmony asked, in the back room of the salon. 'You look really worried.'

Shazney had never been as worried in her life. The working day so far had been a total blur, as she felt lost in a fog of fear and anxiety.

The conversations that previous day with her father, and then Carlton, had solidified the belief that something terrible was about to be done in her name.

Something that would only cause more hurt and pain, and ruin lives.

And she felt powerless to stop it.

'I don't know what to do,' she said, looking up at Harmony's concerned face. 'I don't know how to stop it. We've tried, Harvey and me, but it's done no good.'

'Did you speak to your dad again?' she asked.

'No. Last night he came back late, and with mum around, there just wasn't any chance. I didn't know what to say, anyway. This morning he was out before I got up.'

Harmony took a seat. 'What are you most worried about?'

She sniffed back tears. 'That Carlton is going to do something to that police officer, Detective Cullen. And that my dad has asked him to do it.'

'Then I think you know what you should do, don't you?'

Shazney held up the contact card that she already had in her hand - the card that DCI Paul Cullen had pressed into her hand on the tube train. 'I nearly dialled the number, a few times today,' she revealed. 'But I'm scared, Harmony. If I call him, he'll find out that my dad is involved, and what will happen then?'

'There might be another way,' she said.

'Like what?'

'Call him anonymously. Warn him, but don't give away who you are. That way, you won't risk incriminatin' your dad.'

'But what good would that do? Warn him someone wants to hurt him, but not give any details about who? How would that help?'

'You're right,' Harmony said, trying to think things through. 'It wouldn't help, would it.'

Shazney put the contact card down, and just stared at it.

'Sorry, Shaz, I've got to go back to the client,' Harmony said. 'I'll have a think.'

Shazney picked up the card again and keyed in the number for the third time that day.

But this time she pressed the dial button.

She waited as the phone connected. Her anxiety levels rose with each ring.

On the eighth ring she cut the call.
There had to be another way.
But she was running out of time.

# 34

*Thursday afternoon*

'You okay?' Cullen said, as Marianne met him back at the police station. They'd headed back to where Cullen had been waiting and Poppy's dad was still being held.

'I'm fine,' she said, looking over as Poppy was being checked in. 'Just about.'

Cullen placed a hand on her shoulder. 'When this is over, maybe you need to talk some more about what happened to you.'

'Maybe you're right,' she conceded. 'Or I could just try and bury it again.'

'I know it might come as a surprise to hear it,' Cullen said, 'but I'm not the most open person with my emotions...'

'Really?' she smiled, as the mood lightened.

'But I've come to realise that it really is better to be open and talk things through. Our experiences with Amy, and now with Sarah's brother and Tony, they've made me rethink my hard-northerner, stiff-upper-lip strategy. At least a little.'

'Well if the hard-as-rock DCI Paul Cullen is going all touchy-feely, then maybe I should start to address things.'

'Exactly,' he replied, patting her arm supportively. 'Just don't repeat what I've told you to anyone else. I've got a reputation to uphold.'

'Your secret is safe with me.'

'So tell me about your conversation with Poppy,' he said, getting back to the matter at hand.

'She's admitted she killed Michael Gossage, but I stopped things before we went any further.'

'Poor kid,' Cullen said. 'Let's take this easy, try and make it as painless as possible, for all concerned.'

Marianne nodded, noting that she wasn't the only one torn by this case. 'How's her dad?'

'Still upset. He's really worried about Poppy, which is totally understandable.'

'Totally.'

'You know,' Cullen said. 'At first I assumed he was going to jump off that roof because he knew that the game was up, things were unravelling, and that he didn't want to go to prison. But now I realise it wasn't because of that at all. He was planning to kill himself to try and protect Poppy.'

'How so?'

'He thought that his death would mean the end of the investigation. Everyone, including us, would assume that he had killed Michael Gossage, and Poppy would be free to live her life.'

'It's one hell of a sacrifice to make for your daughter,' Marianne said. 'Are you sure that's what he was planning to do?

Cullen nodded.

'Why so confident?'

'Because that's what I would have done.'

# 35

*Thursday afternoon*

'Are you okay, Poppy?' Marianne asked, as they were all seated in the interview room.

She nodded.

Catherine Cox was sitting next to her, with Cullen and Marianne opposite.

'You understand the seriousness of this?' Marianne began.

'I do,' she answered.

'If at any time you want to take a break, please do let us know, and we can pause the interview. We don't want this to be any more uncomfortable than it has to be.'

'Thank you.'

'Maybe we start with what happened on Sunday evening,' Marianne said.

Poppy nodded. 'It started on Friday morning,' she explained. 'The day I told him about the baby. I called him, while he was at school. I'd stayed off, said I was ill. I thought he'd be happy, after the things he'd been saying to me about our future. I mean, I'm not stupid, I thought it would be a bit of a shock, but I thought he'd be happy.'

Marianne could imagine the man's reaction at being told the teenager who he'd been sexually abusing was now expecting his child. 'What did he say?'

'At first he said it couldn't be his', she replied. 'Because he'd been careful - used a condom - so it couldn't be. He said I should tell the real father.'

Marianne had to stop herself from saying what she really wanted to say. 'And what did you say about this?'

'I told him that it was his baby, because I hadn't...you know...been with anyone else. Never.'

Marianne struggled not to shake her head. This man had taken her virginity and thrown it back in her face with utter distain. She was almost looking forward to hearing about how he had met his demise. She glanced across at Cullen, as a reminder to herself to remain professional.

'And then what happened, Poppy?'

'He came to see me, at home, that afternoon. Told me to get rid of it,' she stated. 'He said I needed to sort things, otherwise it would ruin my life and my dad would be devastated. I told him that I couldn't do it. I wouldn't do it. I didn't care if he didn't want the baby, but I was going to have it.'

'And the what did he say?'

'He said if I didn't get rid of the baby, he'd get rid of it himself.'

'What do you think he meant by that?'

'That he'd hurt me. But I think it was just a threat, to get me to do what he wanted. He just left after that.'

Marianne checked her notes. 'What happened then?'

'On Sunday, I was at home, up in my room, upset. I was scared about going into school the next day, and having to see him, see everyone. I didn't want my dad to know. I didn't know what to do. But he came upstairs, and he could see that I'd been crying. He asked me if it was about Michael. I didn't tell him about the baby, not at that point, I just couldn't. But I told him what we'd been doing - that it had been more than just him tutoring me. That's when he told me about what he had seen Michael doing, on the underground. He'd been doing things to other girls, filming them, abusing them. And he'd visited places. My dad said he was going to call the police, there and then, but I didn't want him to do that before telling him about the baby. I didn't want it to come out afterwards. So I convinced him to wait until the morning, to call them, and I promised myself I would tell him about the baby first thing. I just needed time to get my head around everything. I needed to sleep on it.'

'But something changed?'

'Yes.'

# 36

*Thursday afternoon*

'I COULDN'T SLEEP,' Poppy continued. 'I just lay there, thinking about everything, about what Michael had said, and about what Dad had told me. I thought about Michael at home, with his wife, acting like everything was alright, pretending it was all happy families. I got more and more angry. It was just before midnight and I decided he wasn't going to get away with it any more. I wanted him to hurt like I was hurting. I also wanted his wife to know just what sort of a person he was.'

'You went round to his house?' Marianne asked.

'I got dressed, and decided to write the note to post through his letterbox - as a warning that he wasn't going to get away with what he'd done. I crept out of the house. I thought Dad was asleep, but now I know that he wasn't. He saw me leave.'

Cullen and Marianne were both beginning to get the picture of what had happened that night.

'We don't live far from Michael's house; it's just ten minutes away. I expected everyone to be asleep, and that they'd wake up in the morning to find the note. But there was a light on downstairs. I posted the note through the letterbox, and was heading back home when I heard Michael calling after me. He had the note in his hand. He was really angry, and I was so scared. He pushed me across the road and into the park, saying that he wanted to talk to me, sort things out once and for all.'

'So it was just Michael who came out?' Marianne asked. 'His wife wasn't there at any point?'

'No, just Michael. I assume she must have been in the house, asleep.'

'So no-one else?'

'Just me and him, at that point anyway.'

Marianne had assumed such, but needed to be sure.

'It was really dark,' Poppy said, 'behind the trees, and he was just hissing in my ear, saying all these horrible things, just pushing and shoving me. I thought he was going to hurt me. And then someone pushed him off. It was Dad.'

'Your dad had followed you from home?' Marianne asked.

'Yes. I'd thought he was asleep, but he wasn't. He heard me leave the house and followed me.'

'So what happened next, Poppy?'

'He was struggling with Michael, on the floor, on top of him. I'd never seen him that angry - he was shouting things, I can't even remember what he said. I was so scared, I didn't know what to do. There was no-one else around to help, it was dark. I couldn't really see what was going on. They were hitting one another, and I shouted for them to stop. Then Michael was on top of my dad, and my dad was shouting at me to help. I was panicking. I tried to pull Michael off, but he was too strong. He was punching my dad. So I...I saw the rock. I hit him over the head. I didn't realise how heavy it was, the damage it would do.'

'It's okay, Poppy,' Marianne said, seeing how difficult this recollection was for her.

Poppy nodded, before continuing. 'The rock, it hit him on the side of his head. He just fell off my dad, onto the floor.' She looked at both officers in turn, her eyes pleading. 'I didn't mean to really hurt him,' she said. 'I just wanted him to stop. I wanted him to stop everything that he had been doing.'

'Was he dead at that moment?' Marianne sought to confirm.

She nodded solemnly. 'We tried to wake him up, we checked his pulse. My dad put him into the recovery position. We tried to help him. But it was too late.' She swallowed hard, a hand coming to her head.

Marianne longed for this girl to have a break, for both her physical and emotional health, but the questioning had to continue. 'Can you tell me what happened next? Take it as slowly as you want.'

Poppy nodded. 'We were panicking,' she began. 'We didn't know what to do. My dad tried to calm me down, said that it was an accident, that people would understand. But I was so scared. That's when he came up with the idea of moving Michael's body, making it look like an accident. We hid him in the bushes, went back to our house, got the van he has for work, and took him to the railway yard. He was...so heavy...to carry...it was awful...so awful. We left him on the tracks. We thought that people would think he'd been hit by a train, that it had caused the injury to his head. Or maybe he'd slipped on the tracks.'

'But you forgot about the note?'

'I just didn't think about it. All we were thinking about was how to get rid of his body, how to escape the nightmare about what had happened. We didn't check his pockets.'

Marianne nodded. Everything that Poppy had said tallied with what she had suspected since they had first found Michael Gossage's body - as with most murders, this was not an act of a professional killer.

But the reality of what had happened made things all the more sad.

'When I heard that you'd been to see Dad, I didn't know what to do. I was so scared. I didn't want him to take the blame, because it wasn't his fault. I should have told you the truth then, but I hoped it would all just go away. I just wanted things to be back to how they were - before all this started. I wanted things to be right. I wanted the nightmare to end.'

'I understand,' Marianne said, truly meaning it. She offered the girl an understanding, sympathetic smile. 'Thank you, Poppy, for being so honest now with all of this.'

# 37

*Thursday evening*

SHAZNEY WAS ONCE AGAIN in the self-isolation of her bedroom, still trying to come to terms with the reality that her dad was in the midst of something terrible.

For the whole of her life, she had never felt anything but admiration for her father – he was the rock of the family, the man in the community who she held above all.

Never would she have believed he would fall so far.

*How had it come to this?*

She blamed herself, for that lie.

She turned over on her bed, staring at the ceiling, a tear running down her cheek onto the sheets.

The ring of the phone made her jump.

It was Harvey.

'Shaz,' he said, his tone urgent.

'What is it?' she said, sitting up.

'I've just heard from one of my contacts. I trust what they say. Carlton's target, it isn't Paul Cullen.'

'So, who...?'

'It's his colleague, currently in hospital. St. Bartholomew's. And it's going to happen tonight.'

Shazney cut the call, her hands shaking.

She looked at herself in the mirror, a ghost of her normal self.

But she knew what she had to do.

# 38

*Thursday evening*

CARLTON MADE his way up to the ward, wearing the porter's uniform that he had stolen earlier that week from the laundry room of the hospital. He had really enjoyed the past few days, moving around the building, being present, ensuring that the staff became accustomed to him.

It was a tricky balancing act. Doing enough to be seen but not too much to be questioned by the other staff.

He had the fake ID, the story of how he had just started at the hospital.

But too much questioning would reveal the truth.

He wasn't a porter.

He was a killer, stalking his prey.

And now was the moment.

It was just after ten in the evening. He knew from his reconnaissance that the ward would be quiet. The nursing desk would be manned, but the lights would be dimmed, both in the main reception area and in the bay where the police officer would be.

The curtains would be around the beds, providing the necessary cover for his deadly assault.

Oh the shock they would all have in the morning!

The blood on the white sheets...

He wished he could be there to bathe in the horror of their discovery.

He entered the lift, toying with the blade in his pocket.

He was buzzing, full to bursting with adrenalin and excitement.

The thrill of the kill.

And not just any kill, but that of a cop. It would be a first for him. No matter that the guy was bed bound, unable to fight back.

The lion takes the injured, lame animals with the same ruthlessness as the healthy beasts that require hunting.

Carlton wiped spittle from his lips as the lift reached its destination.

It was the killing time.

# 39

*Thursday evening*

Paul Cullen sipped at the hot, machine-produced tea and reflected on the events of the week. He was only one of a handful of people in the hospital canteen, and most of the others were staff grabbing some sustenance during a short break. This wasn't a surprise given that it was ten o'clock on a Thursday evening.

It wasn't most people's idea of a good night out.

And yet it was Cullen's first choice to spend the evening, now that the Michael Gossage case was concluded. He had wanted to talk through the investigation with his friend and colleague. He missed the chats they had before Tony's heart attack. And with Sarah over a hundred miles away, there wasn't anyone else Cullen would have preferred to be with.

He'd spent a good two hours with Tony, debriefing on the case and chatting about life, before realising that he'd forgotten to eat. The choice at the hospital canteen hadn't been the best, but at least there was food available at this late hour - even if it was only a somewhat past its best but surprisingly tasty fish and chip supper.

A message pinged up from his daughter, Amy. He tapped out a reply, pleased that she was doing well over in Bristol. They were hoping to arrange a meet up in London in the next few weeks, with the possibility that Sarah would also come down for a welcome family reunion.

His thoughts turned again to young Poppy Jones. He had no idea what would happen to her, but he hoped to God that the courts would show leniency. Yes, she was guilty of striking the blow that had killed Michael Gossage, but she wasn't a murderer in his eyes, and the circumstances should surely be a mitigation.

But that was for others to decide.

He finished the tea and was just about to return to his hotel at Euston when the call came through.

'What?' he said, scraping back the chair, horrified by what he had just been told. He was already out of the canteen and heading for the stairs. 'You sure?'

# 40

*Thursday evening*

CARLTON ENTERED THE DEPARTMENT, pushing the empty wheelchair that he had found outside the lift. As expected, the lights were dimmed to help the patients in the adjoining bays sleep. He looked over at the desk, where a young nurse was busy writing notes. He recognised her from the previous days, and she just smiled a hello at him as he passed.

'Just droppin' this off,' he explained, but she was already back to her papers.

*This was just too easy!*

He rounded the corner, out of sight of the nursing station, and turned left into the bay where the police officer was staying.

Again, as previously, the fabric screens were pulled back across all four beds in the bay. He could see the light of a screen coming from the two on the left hand side - the patients would be plugged into their headphones, and wouldn't hear a thing.

The third screened-off bed was in darkness, as was the officer's bed.

He wondered whether the guy was awake.

Awake or asleep, it was not a problem.

He parked the wheelchair at the entrance to the bay and slipped through the gap in the curtains.

The officer was asleep, lying on his right side, his head turned away from his attacker, his body moving up and down peacefully from under the hospital covers.

*Enjoy your final breaths!*

Reaching around the man's head, knife now in hand, he clamped their mouth shut to stifle the screams as he prepared to plunge the blade into the officer's side.

# 41

*Thursday evening*

CULLEN BURST out from the stairwell, chest burning as he powered towards the department. He rounded the corner, and pulled up short at the sight of the uniformed officer guarding the door.

'What the hell?'

The Met Police officer held him back, before checking his ID and waving him through.

The place was full of police. Cullen passed a couple more uniforms, eyes fixed on the bay where Tony was, nerves shredded.

'Please, let him be...'

He was stopped again as he attempted to enter the bay.

'Can I help you?'

'Detective Chief Inspector Paul Cullen,' he said, flashing his ID again while straining to look past into the bay. It looked like Tony's bed was empty. 'I'm a colleague of DS Beswick. Is he okay?'

'He's fine. He's in the private room down there, watching the football.'

# 42

*Thursday evening*

MALCOM POWELL TOOK the call with an immense sense of trepidation. His wife was upstairs getting ready for bed, but he had stayed down watching television, in semi-darkness, waiting for the news.

'We got him,' the officer said on the other end of the line.

Relief flooded through Malcolm. 'Praise the Lord.'

'Thank you for your all your help, Mr Powell.'

He cut the call and began to sob as the emotion exploded within him.

'Daddy, please tell me what you did.'

Malcolm was startled to see his daughter at the door. He wiped his eyes. 'I'll tell you, Angel,' he said. He patted the sofa. 'Come and sit next to me.'

# 43

*Thursday evening*

SHAZNEY TOOK her place on the sofa, nervous about what she was about to be told.

*Would it destroy their relationship forever?*

'I didn't want you to be with Tyrone,' he began. 'But when you were insistent, I wanted to do my best to help the boy. I wanted to offer him the chance that he had never been given before - not just for him, but also for you. I didn't want my daughter with a criminal.'

'I never realised.'

'I didn't want you to know, but I did try to help him. I must admit, I wasn't very hopeful, but Tyrone surprised me. I believe he did want to change. I had misjudged him – outside was all bluster, but inside, there was real goodness and potential. I saw what you saw, Angel. He was interested in going to college, trying to better himself. But unfortunately he was unable to escape from his clutches.'

'Carlton?'

'Yes,' her father said sadly. 'He did not want to let Tyrone go. He made sure that Tyrone stood no chance of getting that new life. When Carlton heard about what I was trying to do, he threatened me, said that he would hurt you. He dragged Tyrone further under, made sure there was no way out for him. I think it was out of spite. From then on, I lost Tyrone, and he went deeper into the gang and their activities. And that led to the poor boy's death.'

He turned to her and cupped her hands in his.

'When I heard the news that morning,' he said, 'I vowed that the man that did this to Tyrone, and you, was going to pay a very heavy price.'

Shazney remembered what her father had said at the funeral. 'I thought you were talking about the police officer, Paul Cullen.'

'No,' he replied. 'I meant Carlton.'

Shazney was still confused – it didn't make sense. 'But the things Harvey was told, about you working with Carlton, asking him to take revenge on the police. Carlton admitted it himself to us.'

'I set him up,' he said. 'I set him up and Carlton fell for the trap. The police just called me. Carlton has been arrested, before he could do any harm.'

Shazney was stunned. 'You set Carlton up?'

'He needed to be taken off the streets,' he said. 'So that all the others, all the young people, could have the chance that Tyrone never had. For too long, this neighbourhood has been dominated by thugs like Carlton. They think they're untouchable. But now they know they're not.'

Shazney threw her arms around him, burying her head into his neck. 'I love you, Dad.'

'I love you too, Angel.'

# 44

*Friday morning*

Carly was a professional people watcher.

She'd been like that from an early age. She loved to observe human life, fascinated by the unlimited range of personalities and looks in life that came within her range.

The man in the scruffy overalls, his cheeks streaked with dirt.

The woman in the impossibly high heels, tottering down the stairs like they were coated with black ice.

The weary family, dragging heavy suitcases, still sporting the airline labels from their recent flight.

The London transport network was a perfect place to practise her hobby, and that's just what she was doing early this Friday morning.

So many people on the move.

Unaware that she was watching them.

There was a certain skill to watching without being noticed. A glance, a flash of a look as you turned your head. A careful stare from the near distance, ready to look away. Sometimes Carly wondered if she was in the wrong profession, and instead of working in a travel agency she should have been a spy.

The London underground was her favourite place. The hustle and bustle of this subterranean world was so exciting, such an adventure.

She would make up stories about her subjects - wrap a narrative around these strangers, give them a name, a job, a destination, a personality.

His name was Stephen.

He worked in the City, as a high-flying trader.

He'd been with the same bank since leaving university, and had been satisfied at first. But then he'd grown resentful of the twelve hour days, playing the markets to make millions for his employers, while retaining a relatively small salary for himself.

And that's when he'd started to play the system.

Embezzling the company out of millions.

Millions of pounds now locked away in an off-shore account.

In a couple of years he would resign and use the money to live the life he deserved.

He would travel around the world and stay in the best hotels, sipping champagne in infinity pools overlooking the ocean.

He would buy a supercar and put the pedal to the metal, blasting past police checkpoints on the American West Coast, with the local rock and roll station drowning out the screaming sirens.

Carly snapped out of her fantasy as the tube train reached Baker Street station.

She'd really lost herself that time, in a total day dream.

Exiting the carriage, she made her way along the platform.

'Excuse me,' a voice said from behind.

At first she assumed it hadn't been directed at her, and kept on walking.

'Excuse me.'

Someone touched the top of her arm lightly.

*Maybe she'd left something on the train and this person was returning it...*

She turned to see the man who she had been looking at on the train. He smiled warmly as the other passengers parted around either side of them.

'We exchanged glances on the train,' he said, still smiling.

Carly didn't know what to say. She'd been caught out this time, and her attention had been misinterpreted.

'I wondered if I could have your number?' he tried, undeterred by her continued silence.

The guy was good looking and confident. She could actually imagine him living the life she had created for him. But he wasn't her type.

Not at all.

'I'm sorry,' she said, already turning to walk away.

~

'C'MON, just one date? We can go for a coffee. Or something stronger?'

Carly turned on the platform to see the man from the train gazing expectantly at her.

Her heart sank.

'I promise I'm not a weirdo,' he smiled, picking up on her discomfort. 'I don't usually ask girls out like this. But, you know, this feels...well, this feels like a chance worth taking.'

He waited for his answer, while Carly just wished for her connecting train to appear.

The arrivals screen read one minute.

She shook her head, chancing a look at him to try and make her point gently but pointedly. 'I'm sorry.'

He continued, undeterred. 'Look, I know a place. You'll *love* it. The food is amazing, and tonight there's a fantastic band on - they're supporting...'

'Please, go away,' she found herself saying, more forcefully than she would have wanted.

The guy just looked at her darkly.

*Here comes the train, thank God...*

Carly turned away from the unwelcome attention and focused on the oncoming train, lights blazing like a welcoming lighthouse in a storm, guiding her to safety.

'You're a cock tease,' he spat, as the train squealed to a stop.

Ignoring the jibe, Carly boarded the train and wished with all her might that the guy would end his pursuit now. Hopefully he would be satisfied with his nasty retort and retreat back into the London masses, with their paths never to cross again.

But unfortunately that didn't happen.

He took up the seat directly opposite her, and focussed his attention on her so fully that she could feel the weight of his stare boring into her.

Carly got out her phone, and making use of the fact that

the tube system now supported mobile phone networks, scrolled through her social media feeds.

But all the while she could sense the man was still watching.

Her heart thudded against her chest alongside a rising panic.

*What the hell was he planning to do?*

*What if he came after her after she had exited the station?*

She risked one more glance and still there he was, glaring.

She looked left then right at her fellow passengers, who were unaware of what was happening.

She was alone with everybody.

Then a thought came to her.

She scrolled back to the Home screen on her phone and found the MayDay application. She'd downloaded and registered for it just a couple of weeks ago. One of her friends had recommended it. The application was designed for woman who were afraid of their safety in public places, and in recent weeks it had gained particular popularity on the London Underground to counter the sexual harassment that women faced on a daily basis down there. One click against the current problem "Undesired Attention" and then a press of the big red MayDay button and an alert would ping to other registered users within the near vicinity.

Any users would then be able to see the alert, view the person's location via GPS, and receive a photograph of Carly, so that they knew who to assist.

Her finger hovered over the red button.

She glanced up again at the man.

Still that glare.

She tapped the screen decisively and prayed that this would work.

# 45

*Friday morning*

CULLEN WOKE EARLY, still adrenalised by the events of the past week. The man on the tracks case, followed by the attempt on his friend's life, had left him buzzing with nerves and excitement.

He showered at five, and breakfasted early in the hotel restaurant, deciding to hit the office first thing and catch up with the less urgent work that he'd neglected while on the Michael Gossage case.

The office was quiet when he arrived, just after half past seven. He noticed that Danny's coat was on the stand, which wasn't a surprise as he was an early bird. He would probably be in the shower, having cycled in.

Cullen booted up the computer and began to wade through the stacks of emails that he'd amassed in his inbox. Most of the messages were just ones that he'd been copied in to, but you had to go through every one so as not to miss something important.

He'd heard somewhere that the more emails you sent, and the quicker you replied, the more you got back. So he was never in a huge rush to reply to anything but the most urgent of messages.

But if it was truly urgent, people would ring.

'Boss,' Danny said, popping his head around the door with a smile. 'You're in early.'

'Winning at life,' Cullen quipped. 'Trying to get ahead of myself.' He gestured towards the computer screen.

Danny pulled a face. 'Fancy a coffee with me, instead? Thought you might like to debrief about what happened yesterday. I still can't believe it. Tony was nearly a gonna.'

'Y-e-s,' Cullen replied, torn as to what to do. He gazed again at the long list of unopened messages, taunting him. He could see quite a few messages regarding the future of Operation Archangel, which were doing the rounds of senior people not just in the British Transport Police but in the Mayor's Office.

He hated all this politics.

Particularly when it involved something so dear to his heart, and something that his officers had put so much effort into.

He clicked through onto the lock screen. 'Invitation accepted,' he announced, pushing back his chair. 'Mine's a cappuccino.'

The two officers made their way down to the canteen, which had just opened, and ordered drinks.

'How's Tony doing?' Danny asked.

'I'm not sure this morning - didn't want to bother him too early, in case he was asleep,' Cullen replied. 'But when I left last night he was okay. Quite sanguine about it, in fact. I think maybe he's just seeing it as yet another brush with death.'

Danny was amused. 'Thinks he's invincible. Like some kind of superhero.'

'Might also have something to do with the fact that they've moved him back into his own private room, complete with armed police guard. I think he's enjoying the attention.'

'I bet. And what about you?'

'Me?'

'Aren't you worried, about yourself?'

Cullen shrugged. 'I don't tend to worry about myself.'

'Shouldn't you be, though, Boss? I mean, this all was to do with you.'

'I think it's over now.' Cullen's reasoning was that this actually wasn't really about him at all. 'Let's hope so, anyway.'

'Amen to that,' Danny said, holding up his coffee cup.

They settled into a silence, sipping at their drinks, before Danny re-started the conversation.

'I met up with Marianne again last night,' he said. 'Second time in a week.'

'That's good,' Cullen replied, really happy that his two friends and colleagues had seemed to patch things up. 'Went well?'

Danny paused.

'Oh,' Cullen said.

'No, it's not that it didn't go well,' Danny explained, seeing Cullen's reaction. 'It's just that. Well...she told me.'

Cullen felt sure he knew what Danny was getting at, but couldn't risk assuming.

'About what?'

'About what happened to her...when she was young. With that coach.'

Cullen nodded. 'I'm glad she told you.'

Danny didn't look happy. 'Not before she told you, though.'

'Telling me was easier than telling you. Much easier.'

Danny nodded.

'She'd never told anyone,' Cullen said. 'All those years, she'd kept it to herself. We're the only two people to know about it. It shows that she trusts you.'

'Wants to trust me,' Danny said, playing with his drink. 'I understand now, her reaction when I told her about my past - about how I'd treated women. I thought it made sense then, but now it really does.'

'Yes,' Cullen agreed. He too now fully understood the strength of Marianne's reaction to Danny's confession about his womanising past. 'I think you know what you have to do now.'

Danny nodded. 'I'm not going to let her down, Boss. Not now I've got a second chance. No way.'

'Good man.'

'How about you?'

'Me?'

'How's things with your relationship? Sorry,' Danny added, before Cullen could reply. 'None of my business...' The usually super-confident DI Lomax actually reddened.

'No, it's fine, Danny,' Cullen said. 'Hey, we're talking about your love-life, so it's only fair. Sarah and I are good. But I must admit, the long-distance thing, it's going to be hard.'

'I can imagine.'

'Sarah up there in Wigan with Philip, and me here in London. I'm just not sure I can do it long term. Well, I think I can do it, but I don't want to do it.'

'It would be more of a worry if you did want to do it,' Danny rightly said.

'True.'

'So what are you going to do?'

Now it was time for Cullen to pause for thought.

Danny's brow furrowed. 'You're not thinking of leaving us, are you?'

Cullen was touched by just how horrified Danny looked.

'Maybe,' he answered at last.

Danny blew out his cheeks and shook his head. 'Damn.'

'Don't worry, Danny, it's just a thought, that's all,' Cullen explained. 'There's a lot to think about. I don't want to leave here. I really don't.'

'That's good,' he said, reassured. 'Promise me you won't do anything rash, Boss.'

'Scout's honour,' Cullen said, gesturing with three fingers.

'Because I'd really miss you,' Danny said. 'We all would.'

# 46

*Friday morning*

'HEY, GREAT TO SEE YOU!'

Carly looked up from her phone to see the attractive, blonde haired and stubbled man standing over her.

'I mean, how long has it been? Four, five years?'

He smiled warmly, but Carly looked back blankly. She had no idea who this guy was. His accent and face was European, maybe Scandinavian.

'*May day* bank holiday, wasn't it? Last time we bumped into one another?'

He looked at her, blocking out the view of her harasser.

May day.

*Of course.*

Carly relaxed and smiled back. 'Yes, I think it must have been,' she said, trying to think on her feet. 'Time flies, doesn't it?'

'It certainly does,' her rescuer replied. 'The man directly

behind me,' he continued, lowering his voice. 'Black skinny jeans, pale blue shirt?'

She nodded.

'I've been watching for the past few minutes, since getting the alert,' he said. 'Hasn't taken his eyes off you. Nasty piece of work.'

Carly nodded, wondering where this was going to go.

'I just want out of this situation,' she said.

'It's over now,' he said with confidence, as the train slowed into the next station. A girl next to her disembarked and her saviour took the seat.

The man opposite glanced between the two of them, assessing the situation with obvious nervousness, before hurrying off the tube without any further comment.

'See,' the man said, bouncing shoulders with Carly playfully, 'I told you it was over.'

'Thank you,' she said, 'thank you so much.' She laughed in disbelief. 'I never really thought the app would work. I mean, what's the chances, that you were in this carriage, just waiting to help.'

'Luck...and the fact that I'm really a superhero in disguise,' he joked.

'I mean, do you just travel around the tube, saving people?'

'First time,' he smiled. 'But I think it went quite well, didn't it?'

'Very well.' But then she thought about the man who had harassed her. His aggressive behaviour had gone unpunished, and he had walked away, free to do the same to some other unsuspecting female. 'I just wish, you know, that people like that weren't allowed to get away with it. Maybe I'll report it.'

'I'm not sure I'd bother.'

'Really?' she said, surprised. 'Maybe they could take a look at CCTV.'

'And see what?'

Carly thought back to how the events unfolded. He was right - there wouldn't really be anything to see. At most the cameras might pick up an image of them standing next to one another on the platform, and sitting across from each other on the carriage. Earlier footage might show the glances between them on the previous train, as Carly had people-watched.

It would all look completely innocuous.

'You're right,' she admitted. 'It would be a waste of time.'

'Don't worry,' he said, noting her deflation. 'He won't do it again.'

'How can you be so sure?'

'He just won't.'

# 47

*Friday morning*

CULLEN HAD JUST RETURNED to the office from his chat with Danny when the call came through from Maggie Ferguson's PA. He had fully expected the call up at some point that morning, to debrief about the Michael Gossage case, but had hoped to get through some more emails first.

'Congratulations, Paul,' Maggie Ferguson said, smiling warmly as he took up the seat opposite her. 'It really was most impressive how you wrapped up that case so quickly.'

'Thank you, Ma'am,' he replied. 'The team did well.'

She nodded her agreement. 'Very dramatic events last night with DS Beswick too. Thank God everything turned out alright.'

'Yes. I understand the Met had things in hand.'

Cullen had been briefed on how, following a tip off from a member of the public earlier that day, Tony and the other patients had been moved to safety and replaced with armed officers.

They had waited until the very last moment before making their move to arrest the would-be assailant in what had been a high-risk operation.

'I'm sure now with the added security in place, we can rest more easily,' Maggie Ferguson continued. 'Our colleagues at the Met are making the investigation a top priority, I can assure you.'

'I don't doubt it,' Cullen said.

'Paul,' she began, steepling her fingers together. 'I know you've been very busy this week, and probably haven't had a lot of time to think about what we discussed, regarding Operation Archangel.'

Cullen nearly laughed. He'd had zero time or inclination to think about it.

'But,' Maggie continued, 'there have been some developments from the Mayor's Office that I wanted you to know about.'

'Oh?'

She pulled out from her seat and moved across to the large window, with her back to Cullen. It wasn't a good sign - she usually did this while imparting bad news.

'I told you the Mayor was interested in the better use of technology to combat sexual crime on the transport network.'

'Yes.'

'Well he's decided to embark on a partnership with the people behind the MayDay app, to roll out its use across London. As a trial.'

Cullen shook his head. He wanted to stand, but knew it wouldn't be a good idea. 'You know who is behind that app? Kenneth New.'

'Yes,' she said, turning around. 'I've been briefed about that. The Mayor has been meeting with Sir Kenneth about it over the past few weeks, so I've learnt.'

So Krishna had been right - the Mayor and Sir Kenneth had been working together. Their collaboration seemed risky from the Mayor's perspective, given the recent allegations against Sir Kenneth.

'If I may say so, I don't think it's a good idea,' Cullen said. 'I don't think getting involved with Kenneth New, or his App, is a sensible way forward. I think this could just be his way of distracting attention from the investigation into his past conduct.'

'I understand that the MayDay app, and their team, played an important role in solving your case,' she said, ignoring Cullen's comment about Sir Kenneth's motivations.

Cullen smiled at the realisation of what had been going on at higher levels. Sir Kenneth hadn't been slow to brief the Mayor about how they had helped the case, no doubt with a view to furthering their own commercial ends. And Cullen could imagine how Krishna Chatterjee, despite his complaints about Sir Kenneth, would have gone running to his boss with news of how he had identified Poppy's father using the app that he had created. 'They did help, yes,' he conceded.

'Then surely you should be at least partly open to its wider use?'

'I'm worried about vigilantism,' Cullen said. 'Now I've seen exactly how it works, I can see the dangers as well as the possible benefits. I don't want the London public acting as amateur police officers.'

'But isn't that exactly what we want? To empower the

public to work in genuine partnership with us, to make our city safer for all?'

'Maybe,' Cullen said, already aware that this wasn't an argument that he could win at this juncture. The decision had obviously been made. 'But I wouldn't be surprised if there are unintended consequences from all this.'

'Paul, I understand your concerns. The Mayor is cautious. That's why we will set this up as a trial, a pilot project. If it does cause problems, then we will respond appropriately, and rapidly. But if it's a success, we have a lot to gain. We could be a trailblazer for cities across the world, a beacon of good practice.'

'And Operation Archangel still ends?'

'I'm afraid that decision is irreversible, and beyond my control,' she said. 'Sorry, Paul. Is there anything else you'd like to discuss?'

'I still think widespread promotion of MayDay is a bad idea, and it might come back to haunt us,' Cullen couldn't resist ending the conversation with.

# 48

*Friday morning*

*How dare she!*

He was still fuming as he exited the tube station, replaying the events on a loop, trying to process what had just happened - how she had humiliated him.

*Had it all been planned?*

First she had led him on with her stolen glances, reeling him in with her beautiful looks. Then she'd callously dismissed his advances, making him feel like he'd been in the wrong.

*While it was her who had led him on!*

And then the final flourish. Her male friend, the good-looking, athletic guy, stepped in for the final humiliation.

He must have been watching all along.

On the first train.

On the platform where he had asked her on a date.

And on the second train, to step in and rub salt into the wound.

He shook his head as he rounded the corner, kicking out at a recycling bin as he walked past.

*They were a pair of sick individuals. Getting their kicks from that kind of thing.*

It reminded him of some years' earlier, out with friends at a nightclub in central London. A group of girls were toying with the men on the dance floor, leading them on, before pushing them away, and then laughing amongst themselves.

One of them did it to him.

A beautiful girl, rather like the one on the tube.

A few years younger than him, he thought. Possibly nineteen, twenty.

Still childlike almost.

The perfect mix of sexuality and innocence.

She'd caught his eye and held his gaze, moving closer in the dance, their bodies touching tantalisingly to the throb of the beat.

Aroused, he'd reached out for her petite waist, but she recoiled and wagged him away with a playful finger.

Still holding his gaze, willing him on, she'd moved closer again. But again, his attempts at physical contact were rebuffed.

Then she'd turned cruelly back to the group, shutting him out of the circle of giggling girls.

A head full of alcohol, he had watched with growing anger and resentment as the group did the same to another unsuspecting man.

He had followed one of the group off the dance floor and tracked her through the gloom of the nightclub. Like an animal separated from the safety of the herd, she now seemed vulnerable.

Vulnerable to some home truths.

'Hey,' he had said, spinning her around at the shoulder with a drunken grab.

Taken by surprise, the girl had stumbled a couple of steps back, but he held her at her arms, and gazed right into her face.

'Do you and your mates enjoy taking the piss out of people?'

She was undoubtably scared. 'I don't know what...'

Fear was written all over her face. But instead of making him back off, he'd felt empowered.

'You might get off on having a laugh at other people's expense, but watch out it doesn't get you into trouble.'

'Please, let me go,' she'd cowered.

He'd realised how hard he was squeezing her arms.

'You kind of people make me sick,' he'd spat, before he pushed past her and headed for the door.

He got out quickly, in case the girl called security.

Out into the cold air of the early hours, he'd hailed a taxi.

'Good night?' the driver had asked.

'Actually, yes, a really good night,' he'd replied, a smile playing on his lips as he remembered the look on her face. 'Best night I've had for a while.'

Back in the present, he headed for the bus stop, the memory of the nightclub encounter cheering him.

~

IT WAS on the last leg of the journey, on the number 53 bus to Hammersmith, that he noticed the girl looking at him.

*It must be the day for it!*

Slightly tired of the chase, but unable to resist the opportunity, he exchanged flirtatious glances for a few minutes, toying with a smile in between looking out of the window.

The girl was beautiful. A lean, sporty, blonde, with hair tied back in a playful pony tail. Very blue eyes, which she was using to excellent effect.

He was pleasantly surprised when she slid in to the seat next to him.

'Caught you looking,' she smiled, her bronzed, bare arm touching against his tantalisingly.

Even *he* was lost for words for a moment.

Man, this girl *was* forward!

'You too,' he managed at last.

'I don't know what you mean,' she teased, curling strands of her hair around her ear. 'My name's Summer,' she said. 'And yours?'

'Liam,' he lied.

'Well it's nice to meet you, Liam. Very nice to meet you indeed. So,' she said, leaning in towards his ear, whispering, 'What would you like to do to me?'

Aroused more than he could ever remember, his skin tingling all over at the words and their method of delivery, he simply said: 'Lots.'

'Can't wait,' she said, pulling back and sitting to face forward. She turned her head. 'Your place?'

He nodded.

It was always his place.

They alighted without another word, walking the short journey from the bus stop to his obscenely expensive riverside apartment. During the walk he tried to process what was happening. Certainly he wasn't unfamiliar with success when it came to the female sex, but it was rare that a girl would be so bold, be so willing to do the running.

What a refreshing change!

'Nice place you've got here,' the girl said, looking up at the block. 'Swanky.'

He nodded. 'It's home.' He swiped through into the reception area and they took the five floors by lift up to his apartment.

SHE HAD her hands all over him before the door to the apartment was fully opened.

They pressed against the door, their bodies moving as one, as their lips and tongues explored one another. He nudged the door closed and they continued their lust-filled dance into the apartment, her hands gripping and pulling at his hair.

*My God, he was so turned on!*

'The bedroom is just down the corridor,' he gasped, in between urgent kisses.

'Who needs a bed?' she smiled, pulling at his lip with her perfect white teeth.

He smiled back. 'I guess not.'

They backed against the wall next to the kitchen area, clothes coming off with ease, not slowing their pace towards ecstasy.

'You're amazing,' he said, lost in the moment of extreme excitement. 'I've never met anyone like you before.'

'Really?' she smiled, arching her neck, inviting him to kiss her there more.

'Never.'

'Not even the girl on the tube you harassed?'

At first the sentence didn't quite compute. He pulled back, yanked out of the fantasy. 'What did you say?'

She smiled, their bodies still entwined.

And that's when the searing pain erupted within his groin.

He doubled over in blinding agony, clutching his penis as the blood from the knife wound spread across his trousers.

'You won't be needing that anymore,' she stated, matter-of-factly.

# 49

*Two weeks later*

CULLEN AND SARAH waited in the centre of the station concourse as the train from Bristol pulled in. Cullen had met Sarah at Euston half an hour earlier, before heading over to Paddington to meet their daughter, Amy, and her best friend, Natalie.

Later they would catch up with Tony and Brenda, and Marianne and Danny, for lunch at a popular Thames-side restaurant that had been recommended by Maggie Ferguson.

Then they were off to a show, with an overnight stay in a West End hotel.

Amy and Natalie passed through the barriers and hugs were exchanged.

Detective Cullen took in the scene, bathing in the enjoyment of being with his favourite people.

Family and friends. Together.

'This is going to be a good day,' he said, placing a kiss on Sarah's cheek and taking her hand.

'Even with the musical theatre?' she teased.

Cullen thought for a moment. He'd been outvoted on that one. 'Even with the musical theatre.'

THE END

DCI PAUL CULLEN WILL RETURN IN
DEEP SLEEPER
OUT 2022

<<<<>>>>

ACKNOWLEDGMENTS

A massive thank you to everyone who has continued to support me in my writing over the past ten years. I write because I enjoy it, but it makes a huge difference to know that there are people out there who want to read what I write! I feel very blessed to have such a supportive and loyal readership.

I really hope you enjoyed the latest novel in Paul Cullen's adventures. Detective Cullen and his friends will return in the novel Deep Sleeper.

Best wishes and take care everyone,

Paul

# ABOUT THE AUTHOR

Paul Pilkington is a British author of mystery, suspense and thriller novels. He is best known for his Emma Holden Suspense Mystery series, which follows the story of a young actress named Emma Holden who is thrown into a world of danger and intrigue after the sudden disappearance of her fiancé. Paul has also written several best-selling standalone novels, including For Your Own Protection and Someone to Save You, as well as the Detective Paul Cullen mystery series.

Paul's writing style is fast-paced, suspenseful, and character-driven. His novels explore complex themes and issues, such as love, loss, family, and redemption.

Visit Paul's website to find out more about his writing. You can also join his mailing list to receive the latest book news and updates:

www.paulpilkington.com

Printed in Great Britain
by Amazon

36874315R00152